LUCKY

SARAH PATT

LUCKY

HISTRIA
FICTION

Histria Fiction

Las Vegas ◊ London ◊ New York ◊ Palm Beach

Published in the United States of America by
Histria Books
7181 N. Hualapai Way, Ste. 130-86
Las Vegas, NV 89166 USA
HistriaBooks.com

This is a work of fiction. Names, characters, places, and incidents are either the product of the author's imagination or are used fictitiously. Any resemblance to actual persons, living or dead, is entirely coincidental.

First Edition

Library of Congress Control Number: 2025944112

ISBN 978-1-59211-681-2 (softbound)
ISBN 978-1-59211-708-6 (eBook)

This book is lovingly dedicated to my late mother, Irene Palatine Rice, and my late mother-in-law, Gloria Goldstein, for whom the character Gloria was inspired.

Gloria always dreamed of attending college, so I made sure her character achieved that dream—earning her a place at Yale.

Irene and Gloria shared a deep love of cooking, traveling, books, music, and dressing in beautiful clothing, as well as buying special outfits for their children and grandchildren. These passions enriched my life and left lasting, positive impressions on my children as well. As a child, my mother made birthdays, Christmas, and Easter magical and unforgettable. As a married woman, my mother-in-law brought that same warmth and devotion to Rosh Hashanah, Hanukkah, and Passover, making each celebration equally meaningful.

I was fortunate to learn from both of these remarkable women at different stages of my life. Their love, traditions, and sense of style continue to shape who I am, and for that, I am profoundly grateful.

PROLOGUE

In the aftermath of my arrest and once I was in jail, I talked with a psychiatrist for the first time in my life about my past. He was the first person whom I believed had figured it out! And he was the first person I ever spoke to in any detail about those memories. Since then, the mental equilibrium I had created to deal with my past is gone. Today, the memories fly at me whenever they choose. They're the first thing I see when I wake up and the last thing I think about before falling asleep. It's terrifying. And I wished I hadn't set bail. I felt safe in jail. It was where I belonged, and I felt like that psychiatrist was fixing me. He was the first person to help me.

I've asked God. I've asked myself. I have fixated on the "why" and "how" questions. Why did I do this, and how can I kill myself? I've never shared the most private details of my life with others in an effort to find an answer. There seem to be both many answers and none at all. And that is why I had no choice but to plummet to my death.

I've had individual conversations with Dakota in my mind. I pictured her face as I admitted what a terrible man my father was and heard the shock in her voice. I tried to tell her that night, but the words just wouldn't come out. They were trapped, just as I had her pinned beneath me. She looked terrified and confused, and immediately, I released her and profusely apologized until the old lady disrupted the moment. Dakota stared at me like I was some crazy person. I lay awake at night reviewing these conversations over and over again. In some ways, I feel disgusting, sharing this truth with you, because in my heart, I still struggle to see my five-year-old self as a victim. But I'm sharing this with you because it is the truth, not an excuse. And I believe it played a role in all the deplorable decisions I made in my adult life.

I always worried someone might look at me and know, so I paid close attention to others for any sign they might have figured it out. No one ever did. Not even Dakota's discerning mother. As an adult, I thought I was a tougher man because of the experience; I was mentally stronger and less emotional than most. I told myself that I was superior to other people because I had dealt with this. But I allowed myself to fall victim to cocaine and willingly let the Colombian drug cartel take over Jennings Petroleum. I am emotionally exhausted fighting the demons that play in my mind.

Jake Jennings

CHAPTER 1
OFF TO COLLEGE

A million things were running through my mind on our way to Rice University. I was excited to begin college, but I would be lying if I told you I wasn't thinking about my parents. I always pictured they would be the ones driving me—the station wagon filled to the brim with stuff I probably wouldn't need but was on the fence about, and Mom playfully hollering, appeasing me, *Throw it in, hon—we'll make room.* I stuffed and squashed my worn, oversized Winnie-the-Pooh bear. Almost every night, I'd used his paunch as my back support as I hunkered down, giving my homework the best-I-can-do attention. My parents, like most parents, preached: *You don't have to be the best, but always try your best!* Before Pooh bear acted as a pillow, I cradled him every night in my princess pink toddler bed— falling asleep without him was inconceivable.

My uncle Travis had won it at the county fair by shooting down all the plastic- moving ducks. I remember the moment as if it happened yesterday.

As their quacks disappeared, I bellowed, "*Go! Go!*" followed by a jubilant "*Yay!*" then a piercing cry as the scary-looking carnie leaned toward me and pushed the yellow bear into me. He grinned widely with his nose practically touching mine. The man's front tooth was missing, and the ones surrounding the gaping hole were crooked, chipped, and heavily stained. And when he said in a raspy voice, "*Here you go, honey,*" his breath reeked a horrible smell, which in my later years I learned was the stench of tobacco and booze. Even my uncle was startled and quickly scooped me up into his safe arms and stepped back, out of the man's reach. My uncle tried hushing me by rubbing the middle of my back, telling me I'm all right. When my sobs weren't ceasing, he softly asked in a cutesy, animated voice, "*You don't want to scare Pooh bear now—do ya?*" nuzzling the bear's nose at my cheek as I buried my face in his sweet, Old Spice smelling chest.

I still hold and cherish the photo my dad took of me in my uncle's arms, squeezing my newest furry pal, who was actually bigger than my five-year-old body, and I was often reminded where the bear came from every time my uncle came to visit, which was frequently, since my uncle lived nearby and was single. Another tidbit about my uncle—he isn't blood-related but was my dad's childhood friend. The two of them were inseparable, like brothers, and my calling him 'uncle' felt natural. For a good three or four years, Pooh bear sat with us at the dinner table, where it wore my passed-down bib as if it were my baby brother. I was an only child for sixteen years. It wasn't until my father's funeral that I learned I had a much older half-brother named Luke. Luke attended our dad's funeral with his four-year-old daughter, Savannah, and that's when my entire world changed.

So instead of my parents' station wagon, I was riding in a pick-up truck, with multiple bungee cords holding down my belongings, with Luke at the helm and Savannah in the middle. Luke's wife, Amber Lee, was in Georgia, tending to her five-year-old nephew because he was about to become a big brother. Amber Lee was disappointed she wasn't going to be there *with* me and *for* me as I opened the door to my first-time dorm room. She went above and beyond, making sure I didn't feel abandoned or miss opportunities that a teenage girl with both her parents would experience. I often reminded her I felt blessed to have the coolest brother and his adorable daughter welcome me into their home shortly after my father's passing. Her marrying my brother was just the icing on the cake.

My mom battled cancer and lost when I was ten, and my dad was blown to smithereens at his job—an oil rigger—when I was sixteen. It wasn't until after he died that I learned he had a son. Before my dad had met my mom, his ex-girlfriend hid her pregnancy, moved out of town, bore his child, and didn't tell him. She kept it a secret for thirty-six, guilt-ridden years, and only when she was on *her* deathbed, did she confess to Luke who his father was. She had also died of cancer, like my own mother. Regardless of my initial fainting at the reception, after Uncle Travis introduced Luke as my long-lost brother. Luckily, he and I shared many things in common.

I remember our drive together after I had dinner with him and his first wife, Janet, and their daughter, Savannah, in their Houston home. He was driving me back to my hotel, and vividly shared with me how he had first heard of our dad's passing. He told me how he had become more anxious to meet his long-lost dad when he had passed the sign, 'Entering Fort Worth', and stopped at a roadside convenience store for water, and as he stood in the short line to pay for it, he spied the local newspaper. It's header — ***Fatal explosion at Jennings Petroleum.*** He knew his dad was employed there. He feared the worst. As the patron in front of him left, Luke stepped forward, placed the water bottle on the counter, and took the newspaper from its kiosk. The article showed a dated headshot of the victim with the name **Jethro Theodore Buchannan.** The cashier commented, "*Jeez, it's uncanny how similar you two look,*" but then quickly informed him, "*The article said the man left a daughter, not a son. Don't mind me,*" dismissing her initial thought.

It didn't take me very long—maybe a week before I decided to try to kindle a sibling relationship. After all, it wasn't Luke's fault that he was the product of a relationship gone bad. Second, I was an orphan. Sure, my bachelor uncle offered to take me in, but I didn't want to interfere with his busy lifestyle. Lastly, I had been an only child and had always dreamed of having a sibling. I believed this was a sign—a sign from God, which no one should ever dismiss.

CHAPTER 2
A FEW DAYS PRIOR

Since Amber Lee was in Georgia with her pregnant sister-in-law, Suzanne, and neither Luke nor I felt like cooking dinner, we went out to Rhonda's Roadhouse. We acted as if we had starved ourselves all week by ordering way too much, but managed to devour it all until our plates were clean. Luke literally wiped his with the last biscuit and plucked it into his mouth.

Before swallowing, he asked, "Do you mind taking Savannah to the ladies' room and cleaning her off?"

I nodded—I, too, had food in my mouth but knew better. Both of us looked over at Savannah, who was masked in barbecue sauce and happy as a clam.

I propped Savannah up on the bathroom counter, wet a paper towel, and gently wiped her cute little face, smiling the whole time. And that's when she told me I do it nicer than Mr. G, her kindergarten teacher. Because Savannah sometimes had a difficult time enunciating the letter *r*, depending on where it was placed in the word, she wasn't able to say Mr. Gloverman's name correctly, so he had told the class they could call him Mr. G.

"Huh? Do what, nicer?" I asked, confused.

"Wipe me."

"When does he wipe you?" I asked again, knowing very well, her usual packed snack did not consist of messy food. It was regularly a granola bar, halved grapes, a cheese stick, and a small yogurt that she liked to eat with one of her old baby spoons, and was meticulous not to spill any—perhaps it was the dainty silver spoon that made her lady-like.

"After I eat ice cream." Then, with a big smile, she added, "Silly!"

Because I should know Mr. G gives the class ice cream. What teacher doesn't— Right? No. Wrong! Ever since First Lady Michelle Obama pushed healthy food in schools, there has been a big turnaround. When I was a kid, I remember my teachers handing out Hershey chocolate kisses after we recited something or another in unison. Now, kids are lucky if they get raisins on Valentine's Day.

"Was it somebody's birthday?" I asked, assuming a parent brought in cupcakes and ice cream so the birthday child could celebrate their special day with their classmates. But I'm certain celebrating with food isn't allowed anymore, especially in public schools, due to kids having food allergies. And besides, what teacher nowadays cleans a kid's face? God forbid a teacher lightly taps a pupil on the back while giving words of encouragement, nice *job*—in fear it could be badly misinterpreted.

She shook her head, "Uh-uh. Just me."

"Why only you?" I could feel my thoughts turning to unfathomable images of this teacher alone with Savannah, and I hoped the look of rage I was feeling didn't show. Before tears could form, I told myself to relax and not get ahead of myself. I had watched too many Law and Order Special Victims Unit episodes, and sometimes my obsession with this television series turned me into a basket case.

"Because I let him take pictures of me." And once again, she calls me "Silly," because I should know this.

Immediately, I hugged her, hoping and inwardly praying that that was all he did, and she was clothed. Please God…

"Savannah, when Mr. G took these pictures of you, were you wearing that pretty dress Amber Lee bought you? You know the one with the red polka-dots?" I couldn't very well blurt out, *Were you naked?*

"No," she answered, and that was all she said.

"No?" I repeated. "What were you wearing?"

She looked away from me.

Trying to sound cutesy to mask my inward screams, I pressed, "I bet whatever you were wearing, you looked so pretty that Mr. G wanted to capture it on film and give it to daddy."

"A-huh. That's what he said." She then averted her eyes towards the basin, looking down at the sink as if waiting for something to crawl up from the drain.

I remembered my kindergarten teacher taking individual portraits for a project. I glued mine down on a piece of brown construction paper cut into the shape of a men's dress tie with a rhyming poem dedicated to Dads that the teacher found in a book of poems. Maybe Mr. G was preparing a similar project. I was getting way ahead of myself, but had to press further.

"So, what did you wear?"

"Nothing," she said quietly as if she sensed something was wrong.

I'm not sure if my face turned as red as the burn I was feeling within seconds of hearing *nothing*. I wanted to cry, *Oh My God!* But knew that'd be wrong. Why scare her? I smiled instead and tried to hold back my tears.

"Okay. You're all cleaned up. Let's get back to Daddy."

Luke was paying the check as he looked up and said, "I thought we'd stop by Callahan's for frozen yogurt instead of dessert here." Then he saw my distressed look, "Oh... didn't know you'd be so distraught over missing Ms. Rhonda's Peach Cobbler... sorry, Dakota. Next time—okay?"

"Luke," I swallowed, reminding myself to stay calm, but all I could think of was my Savannah and what *he* did to her, and *Oh God*—Luke's reaction... Terrorizing. I needed help—help to hold my brother back from doing something insane like driving at full speed to pulverize this son-of-a-bitch. "Luke, we need to talk... and Callahan's is closed." Then I said rather authoritatively, "Besides, we've got ice cream at home. Let's go!" I knew Callahan's wasn't closed, but we needed to get home right away. I needed to tell my brother in private, but I didn't want to do it alone. I was afraid.

"What flavor?" Savannah asked, now sounding less meek.

"Chocolate, of course. Your favorite! And we even have rainbow sprinkles at home!" I assured her as I picked her up, knowing we'd get to the car faster this way. She wrapped her arms around my neck and we Eskimo-kissed, and then I barked at Luke, "Come on. Let's go!"

"Why is Callahan's closed?" Luke asked, looking puzzled. "And why are you in such a hurry to get home?" I was about ten steps ahead of him, almost out the door. "Will you slow down?" he lightly hollered. I ignored the hostess who asked how everything was and wished us a good night. I heard Luke apologize for my rudeness,

"Don't mind her. Everything was great. Thank you," he said as the door shut on him. I didn't mean not to hold it open for him, but I was anxiously scrolling through my contacts for that detective. I knew once I told Luke what Savannah had told me, he'd haul ass to Mr. G's—to kill him! Which we all know wouldn't solve anything. Yes—there'd be one less pedophile in this world, but Savannah would be fatherless. Texas still holds the death penalty for murder.

Luke unlocked the car doors with the key fob and quickened his steps to open the door for me and Savannah. I buckled her in and then finished searching for his name, hoping it'd pop up. And yes, it did. Well, sort of. It was under "Hot Detective." I pushed it to call as I prayed he'd pick up, not his voicemail.

"Dakota!" Luke said anxiously, "Who are you calling?"

I ignored him.

"Detective Michaels here."

Luke heard.

"Detective Michaels?" Luke repeated, "Why are you calling him?"

Again, I ignored him.

"Hi. It's Dakota Buchannan—remember me?"

"How could I forget?" he said in a rather sultry voice.

This wasn't the time to flirt. "Could you come over as soon as possible?" I flatly said.

"Dakota?" Michaels said with concern.

Before he could say another word, I urged, "Please. It's an emergency."

"I'm leaving now," he complied.

Luke looked at me, and now his eyes were matching mine. "Dakota," he paused, hoping I'd divulge more, but I remained quiet. "Does this have to do with Jake's suicide? Did someone confront you in the bathroom?" he asked.

Not even close. I shook my head, struggling to hold back my tears as I felt Luke accelerate to make the light. He usually slowed at a yellow. Shit. I was making him nervous. I couldn't help it. Someone harmed my Savannah. How could this happen? You never think it'll happen to you or someone you love until it does.

It's so unbelievable and heart-wrenching—something you see on the six o'clock news—a child pornography ring—in the hands of a political figure or ordained priest. But this time the victim was my Savannah… my sweet, innocent Savannah—victim of child pornography. At the hand of her teacher, too—someone who's supposed to help demonstrate right from wrong, build trust, and friendships, in the safe confines of a school. I thought of my carnival story and how the carny looked scary and like someone to stay away from, and how *this* was so much worse. How Mr. G fooled us all—his sick self, disguised under his good looks and friendly demeanor. And job! A teacher, no less.

"Oh my God," I repeated, but this time subconsciously out loud.

Luke heard me and barked, "Damn it, Dakota. What in the hell happened in the bathroom?"

"Will you slow down, for God's sake!"

He did.

I mouthed, "not in front of Savannah," and reached to play Savannah's favorite CD: the soundtrack from Mary Poppins. As the lyrics rolled, "*Just a spoonful of sugar makes the medicine go down,*" I couldn't help but feel guilty. It's devastating when something as terrible as this happens to someone you are close to. And suddenly you feel guilty—like it's your entire fault. You failed to see the warning signs. You failed to protect them. I failed to see the person Mr. G really was, and I wondered if my mom could have sensed that there was something off about him. She had an acute discernment of people, even though she preached not to judge someone until you got to know them, but she'd call it *a red flag* if she noticed something peculiar about a person and warn Dad and me. And right now, I pictured her in heaven waving a million red flags in hopes I'd see them.

It wasn't until I became an aunt that I understood how my dad must have felt when I was out late at night with my friends. I had told him, while rolling my eyes, sounding agitated: *I'm a big girl, Dad. You don't have to stay up for me. I'll be alright.* But being the caring, loving, and concerned father he was, he couldn't fall asleep until he knew I was home safe and sound. His answer most of the time wasn't about not trusting me, or my friends, but what the other drivers on the road may do—the crazy ones who drove recklessly. He had shared a tragic story with me about when he was in high school and a drunk driver hit a classmate and paralyzed him for life—something you never forget and hopefully something you learn from. Dad was my protector. And even though Savannah had a doting father, I was her other protective half. The one she confided in when her parents separated, when her mom moved far away and began dating again, and when her dad remarried, with another baby on the way.

Savannah's mother gave Luke full custody of their daughter and moved to Manhattan instead of staying in Houston, Texas. Janet was more delighted in gallivanting with the upper echelons of New York City than in raising a child. I couldn't believe this news when I heard it. I was dumbstruck, in fact, that a mother would give up the impromptu hugs and kisses from her kid for the glitz and glamour the Big Apple offered. My own mom bragged that *I* was the apple of her eye.

So, what was my brother going to do when he found out explicit displays of his child were out there? I inwardly prayed it was only for Mr. G's warped enjoyment.

Please don't have this creep be a member of one of those cults that have a website where Savannah could be plastered on posters, decorating the halls, rooms, and homes of pedophiles.

I felt as if I could throw up just thinking about it. I'd seen this kind of thing on SVU. The episode made me sick even then, and although I knew it was just a television show, I cried. But honestly, where do you think producers get ideas? Real life! And now I felt sick to my stomach—literally. Needless to say, I stayed in the bathroom as Luke put Savannah to bed.

CHAPTER 3

DETECTIVE MICHAELS

Savannah had fallen asleep while Luke read to her, and as soon as I heard her door shut, I heard him bound down the stairs into the kitchen and plead, "Now will you tell me what's going on, Dakota?"

"I can't say. Not yet. Not before Detective Michaels is here."

"What? Why?"

"Luke. Please."

Thankfully, within mere seconds, the doorbell rang. I practically sprinted. Luke stayed behind in the kitchen, which I was glad about because I wanted to give Michaels my synopsis.

"Thank God you're here!" I said as I opened the door to Detective Michaels.

As he stepped in, I frantically blurted sounding out of breath, "Savannah's kindergarten teacher undressed her and took pictures."

He inhaled, gave the utmost concerned look and asked as he exhaled, "How is Luke handling it?"

"I didn't tell him yet. I was waiting until you got here."

As we entered the kitchen, Luke was opening a beer. He took a gulp, staring at me, and before he even said hello to the guy, he asked, "Want one?"

I was surprised when Michaels said, "Sure," because the last time Mr. Trenton had offered him a drink, he'd declined. Then, as if he read my mind, he said, "I'm off duty."

I was shocked but said nothing. I wanted to reprimand Michaels: *What? You're not off duty! The clock started when I phoned you! You're leaving ASAP to arrest that scumbag!* If he thinks I'm being irrational, wait till Luke hears. Wait till Savannah's grandfather, whom I remembered Michaels respected and referred to as *Sir*, hears!

"So, what is so terrible, Dakota, that you needed Michaels here?" Luke said as he handed him an Amstel and added, "No offense, man."

"None taken," Michaels replied.

Michaels looked at me, giving me a go-ahead nod, but with his hand, he also gave the take-it-slow gesture. I was nervous and on the verge of crying. He then approached me, gave my shoulders two tight squeezes as he lowered his head closer to my ear, and asked in a slow and calm voice—very soothing,

"Dakota, do you want *me* to tell Luke what you just told me?"

I nodded, trying desperately not to break out in sobs.

"And interrupt me if I'm leaving anything out—okay, Dakota?" It seemed he liked saying my name, and surprisingly, I found it comforting. He gave me one last squeeze before leaving me to stand closer to Luke, who was now staring at me, looking like I was really freaking him out.

"Luke," Michaels began. He put down his beer and continued in a flat, down-to-business voice, "Savannah told Dakota tonight in the bathroom at Rhonda's that her teacher took naked photos of her."

Luke took a deep breath, clenched his hands in fist form, and breathed out, "How could this have happened?" His face grew red, and I could see the vein on his temple come to life.

"I don't know," I cried.

It seemed like minutes before Luke said anything else—the longest minutes.

"And you wanted Michaels here so I wouldn't do anything crazy?" he finally said, in an ice-cold tone as if he were angry with *me*.

"Yes," I answered nervously. I was taken aback by his tone.

"And I thought you knew me better than that," Luke said, shaking his head as if I were the one who'd taken inappropriate pictures of Savannah. "Dakota, I have another baby on the way. I have a wife, and I thought I had a smart sister. As much as I want to kill…" he paused as if saying "Mr. Gloverman" would turn his stomach, "As much as I want to tear every limb of that… that scum—I'm not going to! Savannah needs me. I don't want her to feel that she has done anything wrong— that this was her fault. Let's just pray to God it was only pictures that… that lowlife took."

Oh my God. I could not believe how rational my brother was being. I was surprised and very much relieved. "I'm sorry," I said rather meekly.

Detective Michaels interjected. "Dakota did the right thing by calling me. It wasn't you that she was judging." He paused, knowing very well it was, but he didn't want this to turn into a fight between siblings. After his slight hesitation, Michaels spoke matter-of-factly, "She has every right to be concerned. This is no time to question what she thought you'd do. What's important is my investigation—making sure Savannah wasn't physically or emotionally harmed and making sure this teacher won't ever be able to do this again… to any child."

I didn't leave well enough alone. "Dad would have killed my teacher if this happened to me," I murmured, not looking at Luke or Detective Michaels as I made my way to the cupboard that held glasses—I was parched. Suddenly, Luke came from behind and grabbed the glass out of my hand, and threw it across the kitchen, crashing it against the wall.

As it shattered into a million pieces, he shouted, "I'm not Dad!" And slammed the cabinet closed, making the shelf shake.

I thought for sure the rest of the glasses would fall to their deaths.

I looked at Michaels and whimpered, "See? This is what I was afraid of."

Then, within mere seconds, Luke dashed out, leaving the house. I didn't have to say anything—Michaels was out the door too. I remained motionless. Relieved, the ghastly scene was over, yet aching with a pang of great sadness. I was proud of Luke and afraid for what would happen next, but deeper than that, I felt the miserable sense of loss that comes when the center has collapsed, and everything seems to be flying apart around you.

CHAPTER 4
AMBER LEE

It was nine AM, and Luke was nowhere to be found. He never came home after he stormed out, but Michaels must have persuaded him into his car because Luke's truck was parked in the driveway. I was worried, but knowing Michaels was with him made it easier. Michaels was the type of guy that you felt safe around if you knew him, and if you didn't know him, you may fear him. He was tall and brawny, and somewhat intimidating.

Since Amber Lee had been in Georgia for the past three days, she had always called in the morning around this time, and for the first time, I dreaded her phone call. I was afraid she'd hear the fear in my voice and ask what was wrong, and I'd blurt it all out, which would send her into panic mode too.

I stared at the kitchen clock as the phone rang for the fourth time, thinking, *What am I going to tell Amber Lee?*

"Hello," I answered with heavy breaths to make it sound like I just ran to answer the phone.

She chuckled, "It's not even ten yet, and you already went for a run?"

"Yup, I had a lot of energy!" was all I said.

"Alright... something's wrong. What did Cooper do now? And how long are *we* going to stay mad at him?"

I chuckled. And wished it were that simple—something my boyfriend did wrong. But that rarely happened. Cooper was thoughtful, generous, and so romantic. Last week, he had prepared a candlelit dinner with my favorite songs playing in the background. I closed my eyes, visualizing that evening, and wished I could go back in time. "Uh... nothing's wrong, Amber Lee. Cooper's great," I said.

"Well then, what is it?"

"Why do you think something's wrong?"

"Okay. Never mind. Don't tell me. But you know I'm always here for you, honey, when you want to talk about it."

"I know. Thanks."

"Put Luke on the phone, please."

"He's not here."

"He's not there? Well, where is he?"

Before I could think up a lie, she blurted, "Something's wrong. I can just feel it. Dakota, please tell me what's going on?"

"Okay. I'll tell you. But promise me you'll stay at your brother's and come home after Suzanne has her baby—as planned."

"Dakota, I can't promise you that. If something happened to Luke—I'm on the next plane!"

"Luke's out with Detective Michaels."

"The detective Drew Trenton hired?"

"Yeah—that one."

"I didn't know he and Luke were friends."

"They're not. I called Detective Michaels to come over."

"What? Dakota, you aren't making any sense. If you called him to come over—shouldn't he be there... with my husband?"

"He came over last night. Luke stormed out, and Michaels went after him."

"What?"

I remained quiet.

"Dakota, why did Luke storm out? Why did you call Michaels in the first place?" Amber Lee spoke fast, hoping I'd answer just as quickly, but when I remained speechless, she cried, "Dakota, answer me, please."

"We went out to dinner last night and Savannah told me in the bathroom... that..." My voice was beginning to crack.

"Told you what?"

"Her teacher took pictures of her," I said quietly—ashamed, and before she said anything, I added, "Naked. Mr. G took nude photos of Savannah."

My sobs matched hers as she whispered in between a heavy sigh, catching her breath, "Oh my God," she cried.

And just as I turned to pluck a tissue to wipe my nose, Savannah was standing there beside me. She was so quiet, I hadn't heard her come in. She just stood there. And when she saw me crying—and heard Amber Lee on the other end of the phone doing the same—she too began to cry and then fled—running back up the stairs.

"Oh, my God. She heard," I said, "Amber Lee, Savannah heard." I began to feel clammy and anxious. The same way I felt months ago at the hospital—waiting to hear if my uncle was going to live or die. "What should I do? Amber Lee, what should I do?" I pleaded desperately, feeling like I was drowning.

"Don't panic, Dakota. Go on after her. Hold her. Oh, dear Lord, I wish I were there. Tell her she did nothing wrong." Then, as she cleared her throat, she prayed aloud, "Dear God, please say Savannah is alright."

Of course, nothing about this was all right, but I knew what she meant. I prayed too that he didn't do anything else with her. I prayed he didn't get naked. I prayed he didn't ask more of her—to touch her—to touch him—in places that shouldn't be touched. I prayed this was the only time. But even one time was all it took to make life feel unworthy to live.

CHAPTER 5
JEZEBEL

When I first met my roommate, I was shocked and, for a second, relieved that Amber Lee wasn't present. She wore a too-tight white tank top and cut-offs. The jean shorts just barely covered her buttocks, and it was hard not to stare. I noticed Luke even blushed like a pubescent boy. She was barefoot, but I eyed a pair of red cowboy boots on the floor as if she'd kicked them off, and each boot went flying in opposite directions.

"Hi," she greeted enthusiastically. "I'm Jezebel. You must be Dakota. Love that name!" Then she took me in for a quick hug, and as soon as she released me, she shook Luke's hand and assumed, "You must be Dakota's dad?"

I laughed.

"God, do I look that old?" he replied with a smile and answered, "I'm her brother, Luke. Pleased to meet you."

Then, when she saw Savannah, she cooed, "And who is this cutie?"

Savannah giggled and allowed Jezebel to scoop her up as Savannah merrily answered, "I'm Savannah."

"Let me come help you carry in your stuff," Jezebel offered enthusiastically.

Luke and I smiled and simultaneously said, "Sure," knowing Savannah would only be able to carry little lightweight things.

"That'd be great," Luke said, "it'll be quicker with your help—we need to get back for a birthday party—don't we, Savannah?"

"Yay!" Savannah replied, clapping her hands. Her friend from school was having a birthday party at the Y's gymnasium, which held a runway trampoline that kids jumped off into a foam pit. It would be Savannah's first go at it.

Still holding Savannah, Jezebel walked over to her boots, easily slipping them on, and said, "Alrighty then… Let's go!" and opened the door, gesturing for Luke and me to lead the way.

It turned out that Jezebel and I had registered for the AP French Language and Culture Immersion class. She, too, had taken French all four years in high school and dreamed of traveling to France and studying abroad. She bellowed as she began hanging a poster depicting an abundant, beautiful vineyard.

"*Mon ami,*" she called, "*assistance... en ce... s'il vous plaît,*" as I hurried over to help pin down the corners before they curled up again. "*Merci... merci ma belle nouvelle amie,*" she said as she jumped on her bed to hang a Chinese lantern above it.

I laughed. It was sweet of her to call me her new and beautiful friend.

"France... China... what other country is this room going to represent?" I asked jokingly, but once the ornate paper lantern was hung, she jumped off her bed and scurried to a box.

Before it was fully revealed, she cried, "England!" as she pulled out a clock that was a miniature replica of Big Ben. "Where should we put it?" she asked as she flicked a Styrofoam peanut off its spire.

I chuckled. It *was* a cool-looking clock, and Jezebel was so funny, reminding me of Gloria, my best friend since childhood. Gloria was also probably unpacking at this very moment at Yale. I wondered what her roommate was like.

"If you haven't already noticed... I am very worldly," Jezebel asserted, jokingly. "And these are all my worldly possessions," she said, gesturing her arm as if displaying them all. I scanned the array of boxes, all opened but none emptied. I watched as she dug out a few odds and ends, like a large ceramic coffee mug with the initial **J** on it, and a frilly throw pillow—again with her initial—that she threw on her bed that instant. Then, from another cardboard box that had the word **FRAGILE** stamped on it multiple times, she pulled out pens, highlighters, a pair of scissors, and a ruler, which she placed in the mug as she said,

"*Voila!*"

"Highlighters are considered Fragile?" I teased, "And yes, I can see how worldly you are." I grinned.

"My little brother found the fragile stamp fascinating. I was lucky to escape before he stamped me!" she said, turning away as she pinned a calendar on the wall adjacent to her desk.

I pictured the word, FRAGILE, across her *tuchus*—one of the Yiddish words Gloria taught me that meant a person's rear end. So far, Jezebel came across as a self-assured, tough cookie—the furthest thing from fragile.

"I hope you don't mind, Dakota, that I'm taking charge of decorating our room. Tell me if you think it's too much—okay?"

I shook my head, "No, it's not too much. What else do ya have?" I asked as I surveyed the boxes by the bathroom door. We were lucky to get the only dorm room on our floor with a private toilet and sink. To shower, we had to walk down the corridor, into a bathroom the size you'd expect in an airport, except there were shower stalls as well as toilets.

"Hmm... lights," I said as I read it on the box. "Like Christmas lights?" Sounding a little weary, I added, "Those may be too much, at least for now. After Thanksgiving, we'll put them up."

"Okay, I won't put the multi-colored ones up now, just the white ones on my Ficus. It looks really pretty. Trust me."

I looked around the room for a plant. "Where is it?" I asked.

"I passed a greenhouse on my way here and want to go back to buy one. You should see the hot guy I saw outside pushing a wheelbarrow—he looks as though he works there. I wanna find out. Oh, come with me, Dakota. Maybe he has a friend!" she ended with a wink.

And I couldn't help but laugh and think of the mischievous times with Gloria and how I may relive a few with Jezebel.

CHAPTER 6
OF MICE AND MEN

Jezebel tried out for Rice's autumn production, the American classic, Of Mice and Men, by John Steinbeck.

"Dakota," Jezebel cried, "I got it! I got the part. You're looking at the next *Wife of Curley*!" And before I had the chance to get up to give her a congratulatory hug, she jumped on my bed—toppling my textbooks onto the floor, and pulled me up from my sitting position as we started to jump up and down holding hands as if my bed were a trampoline.

"Mazel tov!" I cried, "I'm so proud of you. I knew you could do it!"

"I couldn't have done it without you, Dakota!"

We hopped for a few more seconds before I let go, and as she let herself plop down and bounce naturally on my old sprung mattress, which must have hurt a bit—I was so spoiled with my *Gardner Mattress* back home—I sprang off and skipped to our mini-fridge.

"This calls for a celebration," I sang as I opened it, and grabbed a chilled bottle of Dom Perignon and two chilled flutes that came with the boxed set that I had purchased soon after she told me she was trying out for the play. I'd had a strong inclination that she would get the part.

"Oh, my God! How did you know?"

"You've been rehearsing for days—sometimes in your sleep, too," I said, and jokingly rolled my eyes as if I'd just about had it. But really, I was thrilled for her. "Any director would be a fool not to cast you."

Jezebel had worked hard and deserved it. I remembered my parents' preaching: *perseverance and self-confidence equal positive outcomes*, and Jezebel had those qualities.

"I love champagne! *Merci! Merci!*" she cried, thanking me, as I twisted the shiny, foil casing off the expensive champagne. "Dakota, this must have cost you a fortune!"

Of course, I didn't answer, Yes, it did—a hundred seventy-five dollars to be exact! I only smiled and was grateful she didn't add, *Well, you can afford it!* Like many of my classmates had in the past. It seemed like Jezebel didn't Google me, or if she did, she acted as though she didn't know about the publicity I had received last year when I was awarded the largest settlement in Texas for a minor when my father was killed at Jennings Petroleum. The company was found negligent because its oil drilling machines were not up to code. The proprietor was Jake Jennings, and after I won the lawsuit, he came after me. A night I'll never forget.

I was a senior in high school and living with Luke and Savannah in Houston, but I'd returned to my old home in Fort Worth to pack a few sentimental things. Mainly photographs to bring back to show them, and my mother's wedding veil to offer Amber Lee for the "something old" to wear on their wedding day. My Uncle Travis was also my legal counsel, and he had assured me there was no need to rush putting the house on the market. That I could take my time deciding what I wanted to do with it.

Well, Jake Jennings had gone completely mad and broken into my home, knowing I was there. I struggled to get away, but he had restrained me, and in heavy, odorous breaths, he confessed his involvement with the Colombian cartel. He told me how ruthless they were, and it was just a matter of time till they put him six feet under. I had a terrible habit of being blunt and shot back,

"That's what you get for doing business with drug lords."

This, of course, only infuriated him more as he squeezed harder on my wrists he had pinned above my head. Then he went on grumbling about how he despised *his* dad, who was the cause of everything going bad! Whatever that meant. Initially, it was my dad, whom he said he had loathed. Then he started apologizing over and over, telling me he should have stopped him. There were tears in his eyes. I remember shouting at him,

"Stop what? Stop my dad from walking over to the machine that blew up seconds later?"

Jake wasn't making any sense… but most drunks don't. Then, he let go of my wrists and lifted his weight off of me, but rested his elbows on the bed. I remained under him.

He looked into my eyes and softly said, "You don't remember… do you?"

"Remember what?"

"Of course… You were too young."

"Remember what Jake?" I was beyond shocked. He had me completely bewildered.

"Good. I'm glad you don't remember," he repeated with a shaken voice, "Thank God you don't remember." And with a heavy sigh, he added, "… you were only five."

Then, as quick as a light switch, Jake Jennings switched back when the doorbell rang and old Mrs. Turner—the busybody neighbor—was at the door, hollering if I was okay and to let her in. He threatened he'd use his gun if I didn't get rid of her. When I opened the door, she immediately saw how flushed I was and pushed her way in, insisting I make us a pot of tea while I told her what was wrong. One minute, she was consoling me about losing my parents and asking what I had been up to, and the next minute, she asked if my parents were away because she hadn't seen them for a while. Clearly, Mrs. Turner had dementia, but at the same time, she had an innate ability. Like a mama bear protecting her cubs, Mrs. Turner sensed something wasn't right. I tried to play it cool, but she had heard one of the floorboards in the hallway, between the kitchen and powder room, squeak—Jake was lurking.

"Who's there?" she called.

I quickly poured her a second cup of tea and joked that my house had a ghost. She laughed and told me she thought hers did too. Then she said she had to use the bathroom and shared that when she was my age, she was like a camel. I smiled and then politely told her she had to leave afterward because I needed to go to bed—I had an early class in the morning—going on the pretense she didn't know what day of the week it was. It was a Saturday night.

She rebutted, "Tomorrow's Monday? This whole day, I thought it was Saturday. I missed church." Then she looked up at the ceiling and added, "Oh, Dear Lord, please forgive me."

I watched her slow gait to the powder room and was terrified as to where Jake Jennings was hiding—praying it wasn't in the powder room. I stood up from the table and made my way to the sink to rinse my mug. That's when he crept behind me, scaring me half to death, and making me drop my mug. The shatter of pottery hitting the tile floor masked the sound of old Mrs. Turner. With surprising agility, she pounced with the Lysol can—her finger on the trigger— aiming the potent aerosol cleaner in the intruder's eyes as she screamed,

"Call 911!"

Jennings stumbled back and fell against the wall of hung casserole dishes. I quickly took the closest one off its nail and, with both my hands, smashed the dish right down on his head! Jennings was knocked out cold.

The landline had been canceled, and my cell phone was too low on battery, so Mrs. Turner—totally adrenalized—ordered me to run to her house and call the police. When I was fleeing across my backyard to her house, Jennings regained consciousness. He fired.

A bullet pierced my hamstring. I was down. But in a matter of seconds, he was, too.

With all her might, Mrs. Turner smashed the back of Jennings' head with my mom's large cast-iron skillet that hung above the stove. It wasn't until I was in the ambulance that I asked about my neighbor. The medic told me she didn't make it. Cardiac arrest. I cried. Old Mrs. Turner gave herself a heart attack saving my life. I pictured her hoisting that heavy frying pan and saying, *Hasta la vista!* I knew her late son was a fan of Arnold Schwarzenegger movies and had a poster of him from his Terminator days. Mrs. Turner kept his bedroom intact and was never the same when the government declared him MIA. No parent is ever the same after losing their child. I knew she hadn't any family left, so in my ambulance ride to the hospital, I inwardly planned her funeral and knew I had to return to her house to find the American flag that was given to her—she had to be buried with it.

CHAPTER 7
LUCKY

"Oh My God, Dakota! There is a hottie downstairs waiting for you, and it's not Cooper!" Lucky chirruped, reminding me of a cowboy bellowing: Yee Haw! He tickled my nose with the ruffled scarf that he'd knitted. I grabbed it, wrapped it around my own neck, and said, "Until you're done with mine—I'm keeping *this* one!"

"I told you already—the yarn's on backorder," Lucky answered flamboyantly. "It's a rare color that'll enhance those beautiful eyes of yours. So, my dear, it's worth the wait. But if you insist, you may wear mine for today. Mr. Hottie will love it—may even use it on you!" And he gave a sly little shake of his hips with a mischievous smirk as I lightly barked back, "Lucky! I thought you loved Cooper?"

"I do! Can't *we* love more than one man?"

I put up my hand and shook my head in mock disapproval, to stop him from ranting more scandalous thoughts, but I couldn't help but laugh when he gave a pout and asked if I still loved him while he fixed the collar of my blouse as a mother would before a date.

Even though Lucky was from Singapore, his English was impeccable, and his voice was very feminine. Some looked the other way when he entered a room, while others stared because he always wore the most outrageous outfits. His favorite stores were second-hand clothes and vintage shops. Lucky was a Political Science major and relished in modern-day politics, but always brought in the old by quoting deceased presidents—to name just a few: Roosevelt, Hoover, and Wilson. He especially loved satire. Sometimes he wore a top hat that looked like it belonged to Abraham Lincoln. Beyond his eccentricity—he was brilliant, and if you haven't figured it out already—he's gay. Not my first gay friend, either. There were a handful of ignorant students at Rice who believed Lucky didn't belong at the university. I always came to Lucky's defense. I'd get right up in their faces and spit out, *"Who are you to judge?"*

They'd brush me off and tell me I was too liberal. And I'd rebut by reminding them it was the twenty-first century, and they needed to move beyond the 1980s. Lucky didn't seem to care what they thought about him. He'd shrug his shoulders and tell me he felt sorry for them. I loved his self-confidence, and deep down, I believed someday Lucky would become someone of note, while those narrow-minded people would be stuck, struggling at their corporate jobs. But what surprised me the most was that I'd never expected this prejudice in college, especially at such a prestigious school.

Maybe Lucky would have had an easier time fitting in at NYU, relating to more peers, but apparently, he had some weird allergy to the cold and broke out in hives, so his only options were warm regions. He was accepted to Duke and Emory but said he preferred the southwestern drawl, cowboys, and Stetsons, and dreamed about learning to line dance. I promised him I'd take him to Rhonda's if he promised he'd give the mechanical bull a go! Without hesitation, he asked, "When can we go?"

I loved Lucky. I mean, really, the name alone was fantastic! His parents were brilliant to name him that.

Anyway, I hurried to the first-floor foyer to see who this person was, and it was Detective Michaels. It had been almost a month since I last saw him.

"Hey, Dakota," Michaels greeted.

"Hi," I returned as I stood on my tippy toes to give him a quick, friendly, innocent peck on the cheek, and asked, "And to what do I owe this surprise visit?"

"Let's walk," he ordered.

As he held the door open for me, I felt others staring at us—both men and women.

"Let's go to Willy's," he suggested. "I could use a cold one."

Willy's was the watering hole on campus. Then his cell phone rang—a boring, ordinary ring. I was surprised he didn't have something more sleuth-sounding like the Pink Panther ditty. That'd be funny, but then again, Michaels didn't seem to have a sense of humor. Come to think of it, I don't believe I have ever heard him laugh, but why would I? Our encounters were always business—all serious and no play. He reminded me more of a sexy James Bond type than goofy French inspector Jacques Clouseau. Now that would really be an awesome ringtone—Ian Fleming's 007 jingle.

Detective Michaels looked to see who the caller was. "I need to take this," he said, sidestepping from me, but I was still within earshot. "Detective Michaels. Yes. No. Hell no. Yes, I understand—you're the one who doesn't understand." He spoke harshly as passersby turned their heads. One girl nearly hit the lamppost as she biked past, staring at his physique. "Okay. Wait. Detain him until I get there. Make him wait. Got it…" And then he clicked off without even saying goodbye to the person on the other end. He turned to me, "Dakota, that was the precinct. Gloverman is willing to tell *all* in return for immunity."

"What?" I barked.

"He'll abide."

"I don't understand."

"He'll cooperate and tell us the source."

"What? You mean there is a whole group of teachers doing this?" I was confused, disgusted at the thought, and infuriated.

"Maybe. For us to crack *this* illegal pornography link… to the fullest extent, we need Gloverman."

"So, he helps, but who's to say he'll stop? What if he passes a park one day… sees a girl like Savannah and decides to befriend her?" I began to rant, "What if he sees a Savannah at the grocery store, at the library, at the mall… the toy store, and, and," I heaved, "and decides to…" I couldn't finish. My hands clasped my face as I tried to calm my sobs and breathe slowly.

With his hand, Michaels nudged me from the slow traffic of students and led me to a quiet bench in the shade of a tree. Under different circumstances, this would be sweet and romantic, but my stomach turned as Michaels continued.

"Dakota, I know this is hard. And it doesn't seem right that Gloverman could walk, but this was his first offense. We need him to help crack all those scumbags that have devoted years to child pornography."

"I just cannot fathom anyone pretending to want to be a teacher so he or she can have access to children to use them."

"Gloverman signed up for a photography course at Adult Ed. The teacher took a liking to him and invited him back to his place to get stoned. One thing led to another, and before the evening was over, Gloverman was privy to the operation and how much money he could make."

I gaped as Michaels finished. "Like commission?" I asked. "This adult ed. teacher recruits photographers to take nude photos—and for every photo, the photographer gets paid? I bet this repulsive teacher makes an even bigger cut sharing it on some underground porn site."

"Something like that, but not all the subjects pose unwillingly," Michaels added.

"What about unknowingly?" I shot back.

"What do you mean?"

"They don't know their photos will show up on a porn site?"

"Good point," he said, nodding his head.

And just to clarify that Michaels understood what I meant, I added, "A naïve teenager could be misguided and pose nude, thinking it'd be something different, fun, and exciting while the photographer shoots away, filling her head with all sorts of compliments like she's the most beautiful girl he has ever taken pictures of. Next thing you know…"

Michaels interrupted, "She's given a few candid shots before she took her clothes off, perhaps one she could use for her high school's yearbook, a hundred dollars for her time, and she walks away feeling giddy and grateful."

"Yeah, something like that, while Mr. Pervert photographer sells the nude ones for way more," I finished.

"Dakota, Gloverman is weak. He's in debt and addicted to gambling. He signed up for this class because he won a tricked-out Canon in a poker game. He needed to learn the tricks of the trade fast and cheaply, so he took this course at the local community college. He wanted to earn extra money as a weekend photographer—taking pictures at weddings, Bar Mitzvahs—you get the point. This was his way out, his new endeavor. Fortunately, Gloverman just started."

I stayed quiet. Held my arms crossed, trying to take this all in.

"Dakota, I know you're angry. I think Gloverman is scum, too, and deserves more punishment, but that's not up to me. The bigger pervert is this photography teacher. He's the one we want. If he continues to teach photography and persuade his apprentices on how profitable nude photos of minors are, it'll never end."

"So, arrest this pervert photography teacher."

"We need more proof. Gloverman is the only testimony."

"What about the pot? It's still illegal in Texas. Can't you arrest him on that?"

He looked at me like I had two heads. "Dakota, be realistic. That'd only scare him into covering up the real problem. Marijuana is the least of it."

I gave an apologetic shrug, "Yeah, you're right. That was stupid of me," I answered, shaking my head and looking down at my sneakers.

"You're allowed," he said.

I knew he was joking—yet there was no hint of a chuckle. He lightly smiled. And I inwardly thought, James Bond never laughed either.

Then he said comfortingly with his hand now on my shoulder, "Dakota, Gloveman told us he didn't touch her. And he didn't ask her to touch him."

"Do you believe him?"

"Yes."

I nodded, "Thank God."

"Dakota, if it weren't for your prodding Savannah, she may not have divulged any of this, and it would have escalated, so you should be proud of yourself."

"That's what you do when you love someone," I said. "You never turn a blind eye."

CHAPTER 8
HOME

Lucky was going to be our guest for Thanksgiving break, since flying home to Singapore was not only expensive but also too long a plane ride for just four days—besides, it wasn't a holiday celebrated in Asia. To say the least, Lucky was beyond ecstatic to celebrate his first American holiday with my family.

"I just can't wait to devour the array of food, watch football, drink beer, and eat again!"

I laughed.

"I know I'm generalizing, but am I wrong?"

"You're pretty on target," I answered.

"In my small village, we were able to get a few American sitcoms, and Thanksgiving was the one holiday that I always wanted to experience—those TV shows made it look so fun!"

"I hope my family will meet your expectations," I said, smiling. Lucky was acting like a child awaiting Santa.

"Will there be arguing over which is the right way to prepare yams?" he asked, sounding hopeful.

"Let me guess… was it *Modern Family* you watched?"

"I forget."

"Well, there aren't recipe competitions in my family, but yes, there's heavy drinking, cigar smoking, and watching football. Oh, and let's not forget grace. My sister-in-law, Amber Lee, will give the traditional prayer, and then in a *round-robin* format, we each have to say something we are thankful for before we feast."

"Does it have to be only one thing? Cause I'm thankful for a lot."

I smiled, "You are so sweet, Lucky. And yes, of course, you can tell us more than one."

"Oh, good," he smiled. "I already know what I'm saying first."

"What's that? Or do you want to keep it a surprise?"

"Why, YOU, of course!"

"What?"

"Dakota, I'm thankful for your friendship and for inviting me into your home—for a four-night slumber party no less!"

"Thank you, Lucky. I think *you're* pretty awesome, and we're most definitely going to have a fun time."

"I even bought a velour jumpsuit to change into after dinner, so I'll really be comfortable in my gluttonous state. I know how you Americans love to eat!"

"Okay, now you're generalizing," I teased him. I knew Lucky was the farthest thing from ever wanting to put down another culture. He carried on, explaining how an expandable waistband was key for that inevitable leftover turkey, stuffing, and cranberry sauce sandwiched between the leftover rolls, in the wee hours. I laughed some more and clued him in.

"My family eats leftovers right out of the Tupperware—sometimes we don't even bother to reheat it."

Putting his hand to his heart, he jokingly gasped, "Oh, the horror!"

I guffawed and asked him the color of his jumpsuit.

"Majestic plum. It's Tommy Hilfiger and soooo soft," he squealed and hugged himself as if he were giving a teddy bear a squeeze.

I laughed. "If you think our Thanksgiving celebration is huge, you ought to see Drew's Fourth of July bash."

"Is that an invite?" he asked, "because I'll stay if it is! And who's Drew?"

Lucky staying with us for the summer was a possibility. We definitely had the room, and Amber Lee probably would love it. She'd first prepare a welcome home Asian dish like she had a French dish for Gloria's Pierre when he was our houseguest.

Then Lucky added as if he were reading my thoughts, "I would be a big help... cook meals and help with the baby! I LOVE babies and I don't mean to brag, but honestly, anyone who tries my Singapore rice noodles with snap peas and ginger chicken *begs* for more!"

"Of course, they would. I wouldn't imagine otherwise. Let's see how it goes this weekend… we wouldn't want to push our luck—no pun intended." I winked.

"Ha, ha, ha!" Lucky laughed.

"And to answer your question, Drew is Savannah's grandpa, Luke's former father-in-law. He's a great guy."

"I'll be on my best behavior," he returned. "What's Amber Lee's favorite flower?"

"All kinds. But she does think *Birds of Paradise* are very unique," I answered.

"And wine?"

"Depends on what we're eating. Merlot with beef and Chardonnay with chicken."

"What about beer?"

"Luke's been known to finish a six-pack in no time. Especially watching football."

"Has he tried Tiger?"

"Tiger?"

"It's a Singaporean beer. In fact, it comes from one of the first commercial breweries Singapore built, dating back to 1931. Most Chinese restaurants carry it."

"Hmmm… I don't know. Come to think of it, we've never had Chinese."

"What?" Lucky seemed shocked.

"Don't get me wrong, *I've* had Chinese food plenty of times before I met Luke. Amber Lee just loves to cook, so we rarely do take out or go out to dinner anywhere other than Rhonda's Roadhouse. We make a whole evening of it: Texan BBQ, music, line dancing, riding the mechanical bull…"

"Thank God! You scared me there for a minute," he teased. "If Luke likes Heineken, he'll like Tiger. Another tidbit, Gerard Heineken was one of the founders of this brewery."

"You'd be a good person to play Trivial Pursuit with," I praised.

"Thanks. I do enjoy that game. Most games, for that matter. Now, about this Rhonda's. Promise me you'll take me there! It sounds like *the* quintessential place; I just have to experience it first hand—all of it!"

"Sure thing," I answered. And then, for some reason, I felt compelled to share a memory, "After my mom died, *Fortune Palace* was our Sunday dinner, taking the place of Mom's pot roast. Uncle Travis would join Dad and me for Chinese takeout. Let's just say, I learned how to make Mai Tais at an early age. And when Uncle Travis had too many, our sofa became his bed for the night. I looked forward to Sundays despite seeing Hulk Hogan in bumblebee yellow spandex. Uncle Travis always had me read his fortune aloud. Then, after I read it, he gave me half of the cookie and told me I was his fortune. That was our Sunday ritual, I'll always cherish it."

"What a sweet way to replace your mom's pot roast. Thanks for sharing, baby. I just can't wait to meet this uncle of yours."

And right at that moment, I inwardly prayed my uncle would be as accepting of Lucky as I was. I knew my uncle could be difficult and taken aback by those who didn't follow the norm.

As we pulled into my driveway, we saw quick flashes of Savannah. Someone was pushing her on the swing—we saw her feet in mid-air, then no feet, her head, then no head. As soon as I parked and our car doors opened, we heard her adorable, high-pitched giggle, and her bellowing,

"Daddy, Daddy—higher, higher!"

Lucky and I grabbed our duffel bags out of the back seat of my car and tiptoed over to surprise her. Lucky was genuinely eager to meet my niece; almost as eager as I was to give her a great big squeeze and tell her how much I missed her.

And as soon as she eyed me, she screamed my name, "DAKOTA!"

A euphoric Home Sweet Home swept over me.

Luke stopped pushing her and let the swing slow down on its own while he motioned towards Lucky with his hand already out to shake it. I was glad Lucky knew better than to go for the hug—Luke was a lovable guy, but he thought our generation was too touchy-feely. And he disliked how everyone '*loved*' everything and everyone. He'd complain how the word '*love*' was overused.

He had told me about the time some teen had unknowingly dropped a twenty-dollar bill on her way out of the post office, and Luke stopped her, handing her the money. She immediately hugged him and smothered him with so many '*I love yous*' as if he had just saved her from being run over by a bus. When Luke told me this, I automatically defended this stranger. Losing money was a big deal.

"*But did she have to tell me she loved me?*" he'd rebutted.

I laughed. I suppose a simple '*Thank You*' would have sufficed, maybe add an exaggerated '*sooooo much*' to really emphasize her gratitude. I never told Luke this, but I think he had a good point: strangers saying, '*I love you*' to one another was a fad, and it shouldn't be. But like any fad, it'll soon pass.

I dropped my duffel and put out both my hands to catch Savannah as she jumped off the swing and into my arms. In seconds, I pretended to gobble her up.

"I missed you," she pouted, "where have you been?"

"You know where I've been, silly—college!" I answered as I planted a kiss on her baby-soft cheek. She quickly turned her nose onto mine and gave me an Eskimo kiss.

"I missed those," I said. Then I introduced her to Lucky, "I'd like you to meet a really, really, really good friend of mine. His name's Lucky."

She giggled at me and then gave a hyper, "Hi, Lucky!"

"Hi, Savannah!" Lucky returned.

"I like your name!" Savannah said with a big grin.

"I like your name, too!" Lucky said with the same amount of enthusiasm.

Then Amber Lee came out with the baby. Teddy was rolled up in a plush blanket, looking like a cannoli.

"Oh, Dakota, you're home!" Then in mere seconds, she added, "with Lucky! How fabulous!" And before Lucky put out his hand to shake hers, she came in for the gentle, one-arm-hug greeting. It would have been two-armed if she weren't holding the baby. She cooed, "Lucky I am so glad we are the chosen ones for your first American Thanksgiving."

"What?" I guffawed, glancing at Luke. "Has she converted to Judaism?"

Luke widened his eyes and explained, "No, but since she's become a mother, she reads the Bible—including the Old Testament—every night! Wait, we're in for more."

"Oh, quit it!" she said, lightly slapping Luke on the chest, but then quickly kissed him to let him know he was forgiven, and her light slap was a love pat.

With Luke's first wife, it would have escalated into an argument. Janet was so uptight the few times I was in her company. Amber Lee, however, was the opposite and let the little things roll off her back.

"Thank you for having me. It means a lot to me, too. I knew Dakota came from a wonderful family. Your baby is so beautiful. Did you name him after Teddy Roosevelt?"

I laughed, "Oh my God, Lucky. Not everyone is as enamored with dead presidents as you are."

"No, he's named after my dad, Jethro Theodore Buchanan," Luke answered.

"Boy, has he grown since the last time I saw him!" I said, parting the blanket from his face.

"He cries a lot! But when *I* hold him, he stops!" Savannah said with a proud, big sister smile.

The adults laughed as we all headed inside. Luke carried both our bags as he whistled for Cocoa to come in, too. Within seconds, Savannah's dog came running from the barn's direction.

"She loves horses," he said. Then he quickly asked Lucky, "You're not allergic to dogs, I hope."

"Oh no! I love animals," Lucky answered as he graciously let Cocoa sniff him and even jump up on him to lick his face.

Savannah quickly commanded, "Down, Cocoa! Down! No jump!" and the dog obeyed.

"Very good, Savannah," I congratulated.

"Thank you. I learned that in puppy school," she said proudly. And I was so happy to see she was getting much better at pronouncing her l's in certain words.

I was so relieved that what had happened with Savannah and her teacher didn't seem to affect her. The psychiatrist told Luke and Amber Lee, who then informed me that *it* was caught before any real damage was done, and also her being so young was in our favor because she wouldn't remember... just as long as it never happens again. Memories can resurface if triggered by a similar memory—sort of like déjà vu.

Immediately, I thought of Jake Jennings. My mind raced back to that night Jake Jennings held me captive.

CHAPTER 9
THE TOUR

"Can we go riding tomorrow?" Savannah asked me.

"Of course," I answered and then asked, "Can Lucky come?"

"Yup! He can ride with me on my pony."

"Pony? Can he hold the two of us?" Lucky asked, sounding uneasy.

"She," Savannah corrected. "Her name's Merry, as in Merry Christmas," and then mimicking Santa, she added, "Ho, ho, ho!"

We all laughed, and I clued him in that my horse was also named after the holiday. "Let me guess, you two got your horses on Christmas?"

"Yup!" Savannah said...

Lucky then said, sounding a tad frightened with raised eyebrows, "I've never ridden a horse," and then stepping closer to Savannah, whom I was balancing on my hip, he asked, "Will you teach me, Savannah?"

"It's easy!" she answered.

"Not for me," he said in a slightly trembling voice, pretending to be scared of this future endeavor.

I knew Lucky well enough to know he loved challenges. Rarely was he scared of trying something new. But this act of his was making Savannah feel like the big girl in town—the one in charge. Savannah giggled and then said reassuringly while nodding, "Don't worry. I'll teach you," she finished with a tap on his head and then brushed his hair away from his eyes with her fingers like a mother would, and said, "It will be okay, Lucky." She let me put her down so I could hold Teddy.

"Hey, little guy," I whispered—he was drifting off to sleep. "Do you want me to put him in his crib, Amber Lee?"

"Do you mind?" Amber Lee asked, already stepping away, pulling out her apron from the drawer, and wrapping it around her waist to prepare dinner. I noticed her waistline was shrinking back to pre-baby size.

"Of course, I don't mind." Then I told Lucky, "Follow me—I'll show you to your room."

"And I will show you my room and playroom. You can play in it if you want," Savannah hollered as she ran ahead of us, climbing the stairs, mimicking a chimp.

Luke had disappeared, but as soon as I heard the music, I knew he was by the Bose system deciding on the genre we were going to listen to for the evening.

"Your home is awesome!" Lucky said and kept repeating, "awesome" as I gave him the tour, and in each room, he had something nice to say, "Love that bureau!" And then in another room, he said as if I hadn't noticed before, "Just look at the intricate details in the frame of this mirror." Sliding his finger over the carved curlicues, fully appreciating the craftsmanship, he added, "Exquisite." Then, when we entered Luke's office, Lucky cried, "That painting—it's beautiful—who's the artist?"

"No one famous—at least not yet," I answered.

Lucky walked over to the large oil on canvas with its bold stripes across a cloudless sky, gave a hearty sigh, and said, "Leaves me breathless."

"What do you think the artist is depicting?" I asked.

"Hmm... a boat race. The colors are the sails."

"Not bad. But where are the boats?"

Lucky said nothing but shrugged his shoulders.

"I'll give you a hint. It's titled 'Blue Angels'."

"Not bad. But where are the jets?" he retorted.

"The artist only wanted to show the jet fuel. His dad was a graduate of the Naval Academy and became a pilot for the Blue Angels. As a boy, this is how the sky looked to him when he would watch his dad fly by."

"I love when there's a story behind a painting," Lucky sighed.

"Amber Lee's a decorator by trade and likes to support the local artists. I was with her when she bought it. The exhibit showed works from artists who were fresh out of college. There was one that was ultra-contemporary. It was a statue of a funnel made up of a collage of bills. Not money bills but actual bills—college tuition, textbooks, supplies, room and board, bus stubs, and clothes receipts. The artist called it 'Never-ending Debt' and the price for the statue was the total of all his bills. Clever, huh?"

"Very! How much was it?" Lucky asked

"Some crazy, odd number, but it surpassed two hundred thousand dollars."

"It obviously didn't sell."

"No, it did! Some old millionaire guy bought it. He said the artist reminded him of his great-grandson, who died in a motorcycle accident."

"You're kidding?"

"No. The artist was in shock, too. He never imagined it would sell."

"That's so great. Not the millionaire dude's grandson dying, though—that's terrible. I promised my mom I'd never get on a motorcycle. She was terrified of them. Next was the workout room. Lucky surveyed all the state-of-the-art exercise machines. "This explains your brother's killer body. I'm glad I packed my jumpsuit—maybe he can give me a few tips!"

I joked, "*You,* on a treadmill or lifting weights? Can't wait to see this."

He surveyed himself in the mirrored wall, lifted up his shirt, and rubbed his paunch, "This Buddha's belly has gotta go! Will you help me, Miss Skinny-whinny?"

"Of course. I was just waiting for *you* to ask! No one likes to be told they could lose a few pounds."

"You're too kind," he said as he gave his belly one last slap before pulling his top back down. "Most college freshmen blow up like a human soufflé, so why haven't you, Dakota?"

I just shrugged my shoulders.

Then we approached the corridor where the guest rooms were adjacent to one another. I showed him both to give him the option to choose which one he'd like to stay in.

"OMG, I love them both!" Lucky cried. "It's much too difficult to choose—you pick, Dakota," he finished as if it were a matter of life or death.

I chuckled, "Jeez—you're such a Drama Queen—I think you can handle this."

He rolled his eyes at me and teased, "If you insist. Let's see… do I want to wake up with a stallion staring at me?" He was admiring the painting of a regal-looking horse on the far wall across the king-sized bed, made in the softest beige- and crème-colored sheets, and plushest, rich brown paisley-patterned down comforter that practically said: Come hither and jump on me! It was a masculine-looking room and very cozy. Then he skipped across to the other room. Yes—he literally skipped!

"Or do I want to be captured in the array of black and white photographs of France… professionally framed… in sleek steel with red toile matting," he said as he ran his finger down one of the frames. He sounded as if he were giving a house tour on one of those HGTV shows. "I love this one of Notre Dame, and I'm not even Catholic," he sighed heavily as if this was really too much for him. Then he walked to the bed, "And this… this canopy matches the red toile… Amber Lee didn't miss a beat! I love how she mixed the old with the new, the antiques with the contemporary." And as he sat at the end of the queen bed, he patted the ivory spread and said, "This bed feels like it's right out of a castle."

"She bid for it at an auction."

And before I could divulge what she paid for it, Lucky protested with his hand in the air, in stop motion, and pleaded, "Don't tell me—I may be afraid to sleep in it if I know it costs more than my car!"

I laughed. "Okay. And yes, that's what I like best about her decorating style, too—how she mixes the old with the new. My favorite, of course, is this," I said, pointing to the only long, rectangular-shaped frame… "the Eiffel Tower."

"Exquisite," Lucky agreed.

"Seeing that you're having a difficult time deciding, I'll pick for you."

I resorted to "Eeney, meeney, miney, moe" as I pointed back and forth from one room to the next. "You have two seconds to decide," I teased, tapping my watch once in between. "Catch a tiger by the toe. If he hollers, let him go. Eenie, meenie, money, moe."

He listened to the rhyming lyrics with a look of horror on his face. I hurried to end it, thinking how strange it was.

"Moe!" I cried, "I choose you! *Vive La France!*"

He was speechless.

"Deciding what guest room to sleep in really shouldn't cause this much distress, Lucky. What's with the deer-in-headlights look?" But then it dawned on me that it was an American ditty for children. Kids in Singapore probably didn't know about it. I then explained, "It's a silly rhyming song, kids were taught to decide who's going to be 'it' for a game of tag or hide n' seek. Nothing to be afraid of."

"Honestly, Dakota, you really don't know the history behind it?"

"Uh, no," I answered honestly.

"Hmm… It always amazes me how immigrants, like myself, learn more about this country than Americans!"

"What are you getting at, Lucky?"

"While every white kid waits in suspense, hoping the *moe* doesn't land on them, enslaved Africans feared for their lives."

"Huh?" I uttered, completely clueless.

"You always seem to surprise me, Dakota. I suppose it's not your fault. After all, Texas waited two and a half years after the emancipation to tell its slaves they were free!"

"What in the world are you talking about?"

"Let Professor Lucky explain."

"Please do!"

"The second line in the American rhyme, *Catch a tiger by the toe,* has a clearer and more dismal ancestry. Before the popular variation used today that involves catching tigers, a common American variant of the rhyme used a racist slur against Black people instead of the word tiger. Any guesses, Dakota, what that word was?"

"Oh my god, I had absolutely no idea!"

"This offensive variation was widely used until around the 1950s. Some history experts claim that '*catch a n**** by the toe*' refers to a method of punishment by white owners to slaves who tried to run away."

"Oh my god," I repeated. "I had no idea!"

"Let me finish. Other experts found a theory that this line refers to a common way for slave traders to examine a prospective slave. The traders would pinch or twist the slave's toe. If he or she screamed, the trader would decline to purchase him or her."

"How do I not know this?" I said with sorrow in my voice. "I promise to never say that rhyme again." I looked down at Teddy in my folded arm. "It's amazing how babies can sleep through anything."

"It was my history lesson that put him to sleep."

"Perhaps, but an important one, nonetheless. And one I'll never forget."

Just then, Savannah ran into the corridor, and instinctively, Lucky swooped her up and cooed, "And I hope this princess isn't privy to it."

Savannah giggled in his arms.

"I don't think so, and if I do hear her use it, I'll quickly combat it," I assured. "Lucky, I'm so happy Savannah took to you, right away!"

"If you get scared in the middle of the night, you can come into my room, Lucky," Savannah offered.

"That is very sweet of you. But when I close my eyes, I go to Sugar Plum Land, and nothing is scary about that!" Lucky said, sounding so convincing.

Savannah's eyes bulged. "Can I go to Sugar Plum Land?"

"That all depends," he began, "do you eat your vegetables?"

Savannah nodded, still giving that totally surprised look as if there really was such a place. There is nothing sweeter than that magical look a child so easily unleashes.

Lucky continued the litany of questions, "Do you brush your teeth?"

"Uh-huh," Savannah answered with a big, open grin showing off her teeth.

"Nice," he said, inspecting them as if he were a dentist. "Do you read before going to bed?"

"Yup!"

"Do you say your prayers?"

"Always!"

"Then you've got a First-Class ticket to Sugar Plum Land!" Lucky promised.

Now, Savannah's smile was really plastered on her face, and she giggled as if Lucky were tickling her.

"Honestly, Savannah was the one who truly inspired me to pray. She reminded me that the purpose of praying isn't always to ask God for things, or for His forgiveness, but to thank Him for what we have," I told Lucky.

"She told you all that?"

"Close," I answered.

"You're just the whole package—cute as a button and full of wisdom, like Buddha!" Lucky exclaimed, giving her a light squeeze. Of course, she giggled again, loving all the attention Lucky was giving her.

CHAPTER 10

THE NIGHT BEFORE THANKSGIVING

Luke and I were surprised when Amber Lee asked if any of us wanted to say grace, and when Lucky accepted Amber Lee's offer, we were taken aback. We all held hands as Lucky recited a short but meaningful grace. He cleared his throat and began…

"Although I am not Native American, I have memorized a prayer from the Cherokee people that struck a chord with me when I came across it in one of my studies. 'Oh, the great spirit who made all races. Look kindly upon the whole human family and take away the arrogance and hatred, which separates us from our brothers.' Amen."

Even though this prayer had no mention of being grateful for food, I easily understood why Lucky liked it, and I had a hunch he said it often, thus he had it memorized.

"Amen," we all said, but Amber Lee repeated, "Amen," with a heavy sigh and added, "Beautiful, Lucky, just beautiful." We all released our handholds and placed our napkins on our laps almost in unison. "How wonderful it is to have a guest from Singapore… halfway around the world to partake in our family traditions. We are truly blessed to have you here with us, Lucky," Amber Lee added.

"So, Lucky, what brings you to Texas?" Luke asked as he sliced into his pork chop.

"Cowboys!"

Savannah giggled.

"No, really?" Luke said as he swallowed his first bite, followed by a sip of chardonnay.

"No, really," Lucky retorted, "cowboys! I was brought up watching John Wayne films, and as a kid, my mom told me I used to say, 'Someday I'm going to live in Texas and become a cowboy!'"

Amber Lee chuckled, "That is so sweet."

I laughed and stated the obvious, "Not every guy from Texas is a cowboy!"

"I know that now, but as a small child, I didn't!" he laughed. "But even after I learned the truth, I was still attracted to the laid-back lifestyle in Texas."

"This is true," Amber Lee nodded.

"Your dad's a John Wayne fan?" Luke asked.

"No, my grandmother was," Lucky answered. "She raised me," surprising the room once again.

"But you said your mother before?" Luke questioned with a confused look on his face.

"It's complicated." Then, changing the subject, Lucky continued, "Amber Lee, these pork chops are the most tender I've ever tasted!"

"Why, thank you, Lucky. Do you cook?" she asked.

"Yes. My mother taught me."

"When? I mean, how? You just said your grandma raised you?" Luke asked, sounding like a bewildered child wanting a simple explanation.

"My mother was a full-time servant to the prime minister." Then he looked down at the brocade of his napkin as if it triggered a memory. "She was the minister's personal cook. She came home one weekend a month."

Luke nodded. Then asked, "And your dad?"

"Don't know. Never met him."

Amber Lee and I gave a sad look while Luke nodded, took another sip of his wine, and blurted, "Sucks—doesn't it?"

Amber Lee shot a look at Luke, "Language, please."

"Sorry," Luke apologized.

"Yes, sir, it certainly isn't fair to miss out on a dad," Lucky said, looking at Luke in particular.

"Do you have any brothers or sisters?" Amber Lee asked.

"No ma'am," then wittily added, "not that I know of!"

Luke and I laughed.

"Have you ever met the prime minister?" Amber Lee asked excitedly.

"Only once. At my mother's funeral."

"Oh, I am so sorry," she expressed with genuine sorrow, and then heaped another spoonful of rice pilaf onto his plate as if this somehow would make it all better.

Luke shook his head, showing sorrowful eyes, and said, "I can relate to that, too." And then he boldly asked, "How'd she die?"

Good grief! I had never known my brother to be so nosy, especially to a guest on his first night.

I quickly interjected, "Luke, can we talk about something happy? Like, who's coming tomorrow for Thanksgiving?" Even though I knew who was coming, I just wanted to change the topic—preferably to something less morbid.

"It's okay, Dakota. It's a relevant question. I don't mind," Lucky retorted, and then, looking at Luke, he answered, "She was poisoned."

What? This was my first time hearing this. I knew his mother had died, but I just assumed cancer. It seemed like everyone died of cancer. I knew his father was never in the picture. I knew he was an only child and was primarily raised by his maternal grandmother. I suddenly felt a twinge of annoyance that Lucky was sharing his story with people he barely knew, when he hadn't told me.

"Poisoned?" Amber Lee gasped.

And Savannah bellowed, "What? Poison?"

As soon as it dawned on us imbeciles that Savannah was still very much present, Luke answered my initial question in hopes that Savannah would forget the word poison. "The whole gang will be here tomorrow, including Pamela's new boyfriend."

"Have you met him yet?" I asked, happy for her.

"Poison like the apple in Snow White? Did a witch give your mommy a poisoned apple?" Savannah asked, sounding horrified. Her eyes were practically bulging from her sockets, waiting for Lucky to explain.

Oh my God! I rubbed Savannah's back and said reassuringly, "No, no, no. Of course not." Trying to ease her ill feelings because it looked like she was going to cry. I shot Lucky a stern look.

Immediately, Lucky asked, "Savannah, what's your favorite Walt Disney movie? Mine is Cinderella 'cause I loved it when the mice and birds made her dress!"

"Hmmm… I like all of them," Savannah answered. She looked less scared and more in thought, as if she were replaying in her mind what her favorite part of Cinderella was. She finally said, "Gus was cute."

"I liked it when Gus used his tail to string each pearl," Lucky recalled, "When that horrid step-sister pulled Cinderella's pearl necklace from her neck and it broke, and all the pearls went flying!"

Savannah remembered the scene and gasped, "Oh, that was so mean!"

"If you were only allowed to bring one DVD on a trip, which one would you bring?" Lucky asked.

Without hesitation, Savannah bellowed, "Beauty and the Beast!" Then she looked at her dad and asked, "Are we going on a trip?"

We all laughed, and Amber Lee and Luke answered in unison, "No."

Lucky continued, "Why *Beauty and the Beast*?"

"Belle likes to read, and so do I."

"That's a very good answer. I like to read, too. What's your favorite book?"

"Hmmm… I like all of them."

"Yes. But if you were going on a trip and could only bring one book, which one would it be?"

"Wow, Lucky, I had no idea you were this prolific," I teased, "Think I'll join my brother and have a glass of wine. Something tells me this game can go on and on."

"Hmmm… *Alice in Wonderland*."

What? I was surprised Savannah didn't pick a book we had read together, like *Paddington Bear*, *Amelia Bedelia*, or *Frog and Toad*. I knew she read *Charlotte's*

Web with Amber Lee, but I didn't know Amber Lee had read *Alice in Wonderland* to her.

Amber Lee looked a little puzzled, too, and asked me, "Dakota, I didn't know you read that to her?"

"I haven't. I thought you did," I answered.

"Mr. G was reading it to us before he left," Savannah chimed, looking a little sad, "I miss him reading it to us."

"Who's Mr. G? And isn't that story a little too advanced for kindergarten reading?" Lucky asked.

I gave Lucky a look as if daggers were shooting from my pupils and answered hastily, "Her old teacher—you know, the one who had to go away."

Lucky caught on. "Oh yeah. I'm sorry. I forgot his name."

I couldn't really blame Lucky for forgetting the name because I always referred to Mr. G as a scumbag when I vented to Lucky. Lucky called him something else, which was really inappropriate.

Then, agreeing with Lucky, I said, "Yeah, I read *Alice in Wonderland* when I was in the fifth grade, not kindergarten. The books I remember my kindergarten teacher reading aloud to the class were *Caps For Sale, The Giving Tree, and Alexander and the Terrible, Horrible, Very Bad Day.* You know, those classics!"

"Savannah, Why *Alice in Wonder World?*" Luke asked.

"It's *Wonderland!*" Amber Lee corrected, rolling her eyes. Then, from the baby monitor that was standing upright next to her glass of water, she heard Teddy whimper. "That's my cue. Feeding time!" She took her napkin off her lap, folded it, and placed it by her half-eaten dinner. As she pushed her chair from the table and stood up, she politely said, "Please excuse me."

I thought she was relieved to end the conversation.

"Are you coming back down?" Luke asked as Amber Lee was halfway out of the room.

"I'll try!" was all she said as the butler door swung behind her.

We never did hear Savannah's reason for liking that book best because one of Luke's favorite songs came on, and he boomed,

"Let's dance, Savannah!"

He strode to the wall where the volume control was—each room had one—and turned up the music. Then he swooped up his daughter. She giggled. He whisked her off, shaking his booty to 'Joy To The World' by Three Dog Night, swinging her to the beat as her golden locks bounced in the air throughout the dining room and into the living room as Lucky and I began clearing the dishes.

"So much for making a first impression, huh?" he said.

"Don't worry about it. But I do want to hear about your mom. I had no idea. Why hadn't you ever told me?" And just when I finished, my cell chimed. I looked to see who it was. "It's Cooper!"

"Saved by the bell!" Lucky called as he started rinsing the dishes before placing them in the dishwasher. Then, as if he were my parent, he said, "You may be excused."

I guffawed as I scurried into the mudroom, shut the door, and answered, "Hi!"

"What are you doing *right now*?" Cooper asked.

"Hmmm… other than talking to you?"

"You are so fresh," he sweetly chided.

"Lucky and I are cleaning up. Amber Lee's feeding the baby, Luke's dancing with Savannah, and I am desperately missing you. How's Grandma?" Cooper was at his grandmother's in Dallas.

"Don't know. Not there."

I glanced at my watch. "But it's almost nine. She must be worried."

"You are so sweet, always concerned about others' feelings. That's one of the reasons why I love you so much."

"What are the other reasons?"

"Let me tell you in person."

"What?" I said, sounding confused. "Aren't you on the highway?"

"Change of plans. My niece, Summer, has a stomach bug, so Grandma's driving here and staying at my brother's. His wife will be hosting Thanksgiving instead of my grandma."

"Y'all can come here!" I said, sounding thrilled.

"Thanks, but Summer's sick—remember?"

"Right. Sorry."

"So, I was wondering if I could steal you away for an hour... or two tonight before all the hoopla in the morning begins."

"Sure, you want me to drive over?"

"Don't have to. I'm in the stable—feeding your horse a sugar cube."

"What? You're with Christmas? No way! I'll be right there." I clicked off and scurried out as I called to Lucky, "I've gotta check on Christmas!" Then quickly added, "My horse," in case he had forgotten its name. "Be back in an hour," I said as I shuffled out the back door, past the pool, across the driveway, and into the barn—breathless with anticipation.

Cooper caught me when I ran in. He held me in a warm and tight embrace and took a deep whiff as if I were a bouquet of flowers. I smiled.

He breathed out, "You smell so good. God, I missed you."

I turned to him. Our lips met as I whispered, "I missed you more." It had been almost two weeks since I had seen Cooper. He had been out of the country on a business trip. "How was the UK?" I asked.

"Very productive," he answered, before passionately kissing me—making up for lost time. When we broke, he gestured towards Christmas and asked, "Ever been out riding at night? It *is* a full moon. Could be very romantic."

I smiled and noticed Christmas was already tacked on. I felt like the luckiest girl ever to have such a romantic boyfriend.

We decided to stop near the largest willow. We slid off of Christmas and tied his reins to a pine tree. How apropos. Cooper unstrapped what looked like a rolled-up blanket. He led me to the willow, holding my hand, and spread out the fleece blanket. The full moon was as clear as a paper cutout.

My back was leaning against the willow's trunk. He leaned in, facing me, placing his arms as if he was holding up the tree and I was his captor... a prisoner in the hands of the most incredible knight in shining armor, and I, the rescued princess. He smelled so good and looked so handsome, and I wanted him.

He looked into my eyes and tenderly said, "I love you, Dakota." I melted right down to the blanket-covered earth. He followed.

"I like this moonlit riding," I whispered as he kissed my neck.

"I knew you would," he returned, kissing me again... and again. His hands were roaming up my shirt... down my pants, and within moments I was naked. He then slowed down, sat up on his haunches, and looked down at me, smiling.

I blushed. "What?"

"Just taking in the view. The moonlight is cascading over your breasts perfectly, and I just want to capture it in my mind."

I smiled.

With his finger, he slowly outlined the shadow... sending shivers down my back.

I moaned.

He then pulled off his shirt, unzipped his jeans, and within moments, he too was naked, and our bodies were one.

CHAPTER 11
LATE NIGHT BAKING!

On my return from the stable, after kissing my incredible boyfriend goodbye for the one-hundredth time, and him teasing me about how he was going to plan another long business trip just so he could get this kind of welcome home greeting again from me, I was surprised to find Lucky still in the kitchen. The island counter was full of ingredients—canned goods with Asian-typed lettering.

"What in the world?" I asked. And when he turned around to face me, I couldn't help but laugh at him. He had on the frilly apron with hearts and teacups that Amber Lee had received at her bridal shower, which she never wore. "Looks good on you. I bet Amber Lee will let you keep it."

With both his hands in its front pockets, he shook his hips back and forth so the frilly hemline with miniature pink pom poms could bounce. "I hope so! I love it!"

"What are you making?" I asked, surveying the cans, "And where did you get these?"

"I bought 'em."

"Where? In Singapore?"

"No, my dear. I bought them at an Asian market in downtown Houston. Customs usually doesn't let food through, even canned ones."

"No wonder your duffel bag was so heavy. So, what are you making?"

"Kuih."

"Kuih?"

"Little pastries. Very popular in Singapore. I thought I'd add some different color to an American Thanksgiving!" he answered as he showed me a picture from a cookbook.

"You're not kidding—they are quite colorful," I said, looking at the photo of a plate covered in square-shaped, bite-sized cubes varying in color—salmon pink, pistachio green, sunny yellow, and light chocolate. "Was this your mom's?" I asked, referring to the weathered cookbook whose cover was marred with blotches and whose page edges were curled.

The memory of my own mother's greased-stained index card—the one with her famous fried chicken recipe, handwritten in her best cursive—crossed my mind like a moving picture. And then it dawned on me… the black iron skillet she had fried the chicken in was still at the precinct, and I needed to pick it up. Initially, it was held as evidence since my former busybody neighbor, Mrs. Angela Turner, knocked Jake Jennings out with it after he had shot me in the leg. But now that the case was dismissed due to his committing suicide, I was able to get it back sooner than later.

"Yes," he answered, "this was her cookbook."

"Are the recipes she prepared for the Prime Minister in it?" I asked, which reminded me—I still needed to enquire about his mother being poisoned.

"Yes, they are."

"Can I help?"

"Only if you divulge," he answered, cracking a mischievous smile.

"Divulge? What do you mean?"

"Honey, your shirt's on backward!"

I quickly checked and immediately realized he was right. I laughed.

"You don't strike me as the kind to do kinky things with animals… but with Cooper—now that's another story! Now tell me everything and don't leave anything out!"

I blushed.

"Oh, quit being so innocent."

"How'd ya know?"

"I saw his car when I took out the trash!"

I smiled. "Cooper told me to tell you hello from him and that he's looking forward to Friday night."

He gave a smile as if he were just asked to dance by a cute boy and then said, "Friday night?" looking confused.

"Yeah, isn't that when you're making your ginger chicken with snap peas and rice noodles specialty? I invited him over."

"I thought I'd do it Saturday night. And I'm going to substitute the chicken with shrimp since we're having a twenty-pound turkey tomorrow night! I saw it in the fridge. That thing's huge. How many people are coming over again?"

"Five plus us six, but Timmy's on formula, and Savannah and her friend Alexis eat like mice, so really eight adults who will devour Luke's toddler-size turkey."

He laughed. "Oh, I am so looking forward to meeting everyone. Is Alexis as cute as Savannah?"

"Yes, but quieter. She's shy at first but comes around. Oh, and her mom, Pamela, has a new boyfriend."

"Your brother mentioned he's coming—did you include him in your count?"

"No. You're keen, Lucky," I said with a wink.

"So, it'll be nine adults?"

"Yes!"

"Well, I have my work cut out for me. I'll get Alexis giggling in no time and Pamela to divulge something juicy about her new beau. Where's Alexis' dad?" Lucky asked.

"In prison."

Lucky looked aghast. "Really?" he said with a hand to his chest.

"Really," I answered. "Caught transporting cocaine."

"Oh, my God. And Pamela had no clue?"

"No. And for obvious reasons, Alexis isn't privy to any of this."

"Has she ever asked where her daddy is?"

"I think Pamela just told her he is gone. Honestly, I'm not really sure."

"That must be so difficult for Pamela."

"Agreed. On a lighter note, remember, Saturday night you're going to ride the mechanical bull!" I reminded him.

"Yes! At Rhonda's Rodeo Roadhouse!" Lucky confirmed. "How could I forget? And I'm going to learn *the* ultimate country western dance, too? Hey, can Cooper come?"

"He's *my* boyfriend! And yes, he plans to, unless he has to drive his grandmother home, but I'm sure she's going to stay longer to help out since her granddaughter, Summer, is sick. That's how I got to see him tonight," I said, smiling.

"The poor child's sick and you're smiling!" Lucky shook his head, giving a "tsk, tsk" as he threw a dish towel at my dreamy appearance.

I suddenly had a memory of my dad's funeral when my Uncle Travis eyed me, smiling, and asked me what was so amusing. I inwardly was reminiscing about my mom and dad's loving moments and had pictured the two of them in Heaven's kitchen—her at the oven taking out hot biscuits and his hand cupping her derriere! Her scolding, '*Quit your foolin', Jethro, this here's piping hot!*' But relishing in his touch as he whispered in her ear, '*I love you.*'

"Hello! Anybody in there?" Lucky said while giving my head two light knocks. "Back to earth, Dakota!" he teased in a Martian accent.

"You know what I mean. Of course, I feel sorry for the kid. I'm just happy I got to see Cooper—that's all."

"Okay. Don't rub it in. Some of us aren't lucky enough to have a heartthrob partner! Now go wash your hands, put on an apron, and I'll tell you what to do!" Lucky instructed like a Home Ec. teacher.

There is something about shared labor that makes people more easily open up, and while he opened the can of coconut milk and I unwrapped the squares of bittersweet chocolate, he told me about his mother's passing.

"I remember," Lucky began, concentrating on opening the can, "I remember," he repeated, "sitting as an adolescent boy on the butcher block at the center of the kitchen, being very careful eating slices of mango with a fork—dreaming of when I could fly to America—Grandma didn't want me to get any on my clothes, especially on this particular day."

"Why?"

"Oh, she was a clean freak."

"No, not that. What was so special about this day that you had to keep clean?"

"It was my mother's funeral."

"I'm sorry. How old were you when she died?"

"Twelve."

He poured the coconut milk into the mixing bowl and then walked over to the sink to rinse out the empty can, gave it two shakes upside down over the sink, walked toward the recycle bin, stopped mid-way, and shot it in.

I cheered, "Three-pointer!"

"Have you heard of pufferfish?" he asked.

"Yeah, they're poisonous. You don't eat 'em, that's for sure."

"Well, they're a delicacy in Asia for the very affluent, but it takes a trained and very meticulous person to cut out all the venom before serving it." And with a heavy sigh, he revealed, "Or else the diner dies."

I nodded with bulging eyes, somewhat scared of what Lucky was going to say next.

"The Prime Minister that evening felt ill and declined dinner. He went straight to his room, asking for a pot of tea and a heated blanket. His wishes were granted, and my mother brought home the pufferfish dinner she had prepared for him. Fish was something you never reheated and served the next day. We always got the leftovers on the Friday she returned home for that one weekend a month. She spent the other three weekends at the prime minister's because he had to host either big galas or small, intimate parties that usually fell on a Saturday, and regardless of the guest count, he needed her to cook. Grandma and I had already eaten dinner on that particular Friday because Grandma misunderstood and thought my mom told her it was the following weekend she'd return home, or else we would have waited to eat dinner with her. We did, however, devour the dessert she had brought home—a creamy caramel custard—before she even changed out of her uniform. My mom saw the table set for Mahjong, and the old lady who lived next to us was impatiently waiting. She was the third player, and had we known Mom was coming home, we would never have invited her over. Do you know the game Mahjong?"

"I've seen it played when my mom volunteered at an assisted living home, and I tagged along. It's played with tiles similar to American Rummy Cube—right?"

"Yup. And you need a minimum of three people to play."

"But it's better with four players. Why didn't your mom play with you guys?"

"She didn't care for Foo Foo—that was the old lady. We had to keep a close eye on her because she had a reputation for cheating. So, as our fingers turned tiles, my mother sat in the adjacent kitchen—only a silk screen separated the two rooms. Foo Foo asked for a pot of tea. Grandma looked at me to get it. We both couldn't leave in case the old woman switched a tile. Grandma could argue with Foo Foo if she believed the hag was dishonest. Whereas, the young—me—are never supposed to raise their voice to their elders—never! I didn't stand a chance if I caught her cheating—I had to keep my mouth shut. So, I got up to put on the kettle and that's when I saw my mother's face lying on her plate."

I gasped with both my hands to my mouth, looking utterly shocked, and said, "Oh my god—she didn't remove all the poison!"

"It wasn't her job to. It was the fish market's job. My mom was to prepare it for cooking only," he said, shaking his head while cracking an egg. I was surprised he could multitask while telling me this devastating story.

"Oh my god, that means somebody wanted the prime minister dead!"

"Yup!"

"Did he do something?"

"Vamped up security."

"No, about your mother?

"There was nothing he could do."

"Yeah, but what about you? You were a child without a mother. Did he sue the fish market?"

He laughed. "That's so American. Doesn't work like that where I come from, especially when my mother was of the working class—granted, she was in a higher sect because of *where* she worked. Anyway, the tiny market in my village is a one-man shop. He did stop selling puffer fish after my mom died."

"That's all?"

"Yup. Suing is not a pastime in Asia like it is in America. Let me continue. The poison causes a person to go into cardiac arrest, so when the news spread of her death, it said the prime minister's cook had died of a heart attack. Unfortunately, Singapore doesn't sensationalize like America does—no offense. She was easily replaced and forgotten within days of her funeral.

I gasped. "I had no idea. Just think if you and your grandma weren't already full—the three—maybe four of you, if Foo Foo ate—would be dead, too."

Lucky nodded, "I know."

"How's your grandma coping?"

"She died two weeks before I flew here."

I gasped and held my heart, but said nothing. I had no idea.

"So, since I've never met my dad and have no clue as to where he is or if he's even still alive, and my mom's in heaven—I consider myself an orphan."

"Oh, Lucky," I said with a pout, "I am so sorry."

"Honestly, Dakota. My grandma was very old and, although she encouraged me to come to America, I knew deep down it'd kill her. But she insisted, especially when I received a scholarship to Rice. Her dying before I left was a blessing. It was almost like she planned it, too. Every day, she'd hobble to the town's sanctuary and kneel across from Buddha and pray. She even had written a personal, three-page letter to me with her wishes and funeral instructions, and money. All her life savings were tightly rolled into a ginger jar under one of the floorboards next to our family altar."

CHAPTER 12
TURKEY DAY!

Considering Lucky and I didn't get to bed until one in the morning, we still managed to wake up at nine. I wouldn't dare complain about not being able to sleep in any way, considering it was Luke and Amber Lee who were up around the clock with Teddy. But last night the baby slept for five straight hours, which was a big deal, and this put Amber Lee in a better mood—on top of her already bubbly self. When she eyed the array of little cakes Lucky had arranged nicely on three different platters, she was pleasantly surprised and very touched that he had contributed to the dessert table. And, surprising us all, she knew exactly what they were! This impressed Lucky tremendously.

"Alright, now that you both managed to surprise one another, can I get some help putting the table leaves in?" Luke asked. "Company will be here at two."

Amber Lee seemed pretty well organized—she had written a To Do list on the large blackboard that took up a quarter of a wall in the kitchen, and already most of it was checked off.

"I'll help you, Luke," I answered.

"Tell me what you want me to do," Lucky said, looking at Amber Lee.

Savannah was in her playroom, and Teddy was taking his morning nap—he had been up since six.

"We'll set the table, too," Luke called from the dining room. I popped my head out from behind the swinging butler door back at Amber Lee and teased, "Don't worry, you can fix and rearrange—we won't be offended." Knowing very well, Amber Lee had a certain way she liked the table formally set.

She smiled, gave a quick, "Thanks!" and then returned to watching Lucky as if he were her apprentice.

When Luke and I were through, I called up to Savannah, "Time to make your famous apple cake!"

She must have been already making her way down the steps because within seconds, Savannah was on top of me! I caught her and kissed her. She told me to hold still as she gently returned my kiss with a butterfly kiss.

I giggled, "It tickles!" as her long eyelashes swept gently across my cheek like a butterfly's wings. "Thank you!" I said as I carried Savannah over to an empty spot on the counter and put her down. "Do you remember all the ingredients in your famous cake, Savannah?" as if she invented it. She nodded but didn't get the hint of actually listing them. I smiled and retrieved the *Joy of Cooking* cookbook from the shelf below her dangling feet, and found the page bookmarked with one of Savannah's drawings.

As I unfolded it, she said, remembering, "I made that for Hubbell. He forgot it."

"Oh," I said. Not sure if her feelings were hurt about my former boyfriend, Hubbel, leaving the picture she made for him behind, which he probably did intentionally.

"Oh well," she said, "it makes a good bookmark!" And I smiled at her optimism, thinking that if everyone could adopt this positive attitude, life could be less stressful and more meaningful.

"You can give it to Cooper if you want?" I suggested.

"No way! He gets a fresh one. What do you think I was doing all morning?" she said all matter-of-factly as I stared at her amazing self. "I was painting in my playroom!" she continued with animated arms.

My parents used to chuckle when I'd talk with my hands too, and commented how there wasn't an ounce of Italian in me, but one would think I was from Sicily.

"Wait till you see what I made him! I hope he likes blue and green."

I smiled and said, "Miss Savannah, you are just too cute! I love you more and more every day. And whatever color you used for one of your masterpieces— Cooper's going to love it! I bet he'll even frame it!"

I put her hair back and tied her Polly Pocket apron around her teeny waist. We washed our hands together at the smaller sink and then began the cake process.

Luke checked off "Set Up Bar" on the board and went to it, as his daughter corrected, "Dad, you don't check it off before you do it. You check it off after you do it!"

He grunted.

"Somebody's cranky," I mumbled.

"I've got an idea—you and Lucky take the night shift and see how it feels," he said, slightly agitated.

Lucky volunteered, "We'd love to!"

Amber Lee chimed in, "Of course, we wouldn't have our guest do that. Luke was just kidding."

"I don't think so," I answered as Luke had already left for the den/billiard room where the bar was.

He had to make sure there was enough ice, cold beer, at least two bottles of chilled white wine, red wine, clean glasses, fresh cut limes for Pamela's vodka Cosmos, Roquefort-filled olives for Crystal's gin martini, and of course, he had to double check if Drew and Travis' choice of scotch was on hand. It usually was, since Luke rarely touched it—it was basically their personal stock.

Amber Lee was searching the cupboards. Opening and closing the doors as she talked to herself aloud, "Think, Amber Lee, where did you put them?"

"Mom, what are you looking for?" Savannah asked.

And at that moment, Amber Lee stopped what she was doing, sure-footed her way over to Savannah, took her little face in her hands, kissed it, looked straight into her eyes, and said, "I love you!" Then she kissed the top of Savannah's head and held it still with one hand so she wouldn't bump it on the door of the cupboard that she searched with the other hand, moving stuff around.

Amber Lee absolutely loved it when Savannah called her, "Mom." She called her real mom "Mom" too. Savannah was the most easy-going child.

"Well?" Savannah asked again as Amber Lee closed the cabinet and habitually planted another peck on her stepdaughter's crown.

"Oh. I bought these darling little turkey toothpicks for the bar and hors d'oeuvres. I thought it'd be cute if Luke stabbed one in the blue cheese olives for Crystal's martini!" she answered.

"Oh," Savannah said, sounding guilty. "I used them for my project. They're up in my playroom."

Not sounding upset in the least bit, Amber Lee asked, "Are there any left, or did you use them all?"

"I think there are a few left. I go get 'em," she answered as I helped her down. "I'll bring what I made with them down, too," she bellowed as she climbed the steps. Simultaneously, Teddy's cry came over the monitor that Amber Lee had clasped to her apron.

"And I'll bring down the baby," Lucky volunteered as he followed Savannah up the stairs, calling back down, "You can hear me through the monitor if he takes to me or not."

Amber Lee and I laughed, and within minutes we heard Lucky through the baby monitor cooing, "Hey little fella—Lucky's going to carry you to your mama."

Then we heard Savannah, "Mom changes his diaper when he wakes up. You have to change his diaper, Lucky!"

Then Lucky spoke into the monitor, "Houston, we have a problem. I have never changed a baby's diaper! Houston—do you read me?" Adding, "Over," even though the baby monitor wasn't a two-way transmitter. But I'm not quite sure Lucky knew that because a worried-sounding, "Well?" came through seconds later.

Amber Lee and I were rolling. Luke too. He had just returned to the kitchen when Lucky was giving his Apollo 13 movie rendition.

"I'm on my way," Luke said without hesitation, trotting up the stairs, taking two at a time.

The four of them descended about five minutes later. Savannah was carefully carrying a tray with a turkey on it. More specifically, the tray was makeshift from a cereal box, with a mound of Play-Doh molded into an oval-shaped ball, and a shorter one at the end, which I assumed was intended to be the turkey's neck. It must have collapsed, so Savannah compromised, making it stout so it'd stay in place. It had multicolored feathers sticking from its rear, looking more like a pea-cock caged in by a decorative toothpick fence. As Savannah gingerly placed it down on the kitchen table, she took a handful of the leftover toothpicks with gold paper turkey heads from her pocket and handed them to Amber Lee.

"Sure you don't need 'em?" Amber Lee asked before collecting them from Savannah's tiny palm.

"No. I think Mr. Turkey is fenced in enough," she answered.

"Yes, I think so, too. Let's use him on the dessert table as the centerpiece."

"Okay. But I hope nobody thinks he's dessert, and eats him!" We laughed, but Savannah was serious and asked, "What's so funny?"

"You are!" Luke answered. "What dessert have you seen, honey, that has feathers sticking from it?" he asked while picking her up and kissing her. "And it's a little too big to be made of marzipan," he added.

"Holy cow! You know marzipan, but you didn't know challah?" I cried.

Amber Lee chuckled, agreeing with me, "Oh, honey, you always seem to surprise me!"

When my childhood friend, Gloria, visited and stayed with us, she made French toast for breakfast with challah, and Luke loved it. He practically savored each bite and in between his mmm…mm's he referred to it as the best "holly" French toast, and then when he saw our "what?" look, he corrected, "I mean holy French toast" and then when we shot him another unbelievable look, he pleaded, "Will you leave a man in peace to enjoy his breakfast!"

I remember that morning as if it were yesterday. Gloria slowly explained to Luke as if he were inept, holding up the other, unused loaf of challah she had brought as part of her hostess gift.

"This here braided bread—challah," she enunciated clearly, "is a leavened bread traditionally baked to celebrate the Jewish sabbath and Jewish holidays such as Rosh Hashanah—the Jewish New Year—but never Passover!"

Luke looked and questioned, "Passover?"

"Oy!" she had said with rolled eyes. "I'll ask my parents to invite y'all! It'll be a seder you won't forget."

Again, Luke looked lost. Amber Lee and I laughed.

Lucky had the baby cradled in his arms and asked, not looking up from Teddy's angelic face, "Can I give him his bottle?" Lucky was transfixed. "He is so beautiful."

"That would be lovely," Amber Lee replied, walking to the fridge that held a bottle of breast milk she had pumped earlier. "Let me just zap this for a few seconds to get the chill out," she said as she placed the bottle in the microwave and punched in numbers. A moment later, Lucky declared he was in heaven as he took a seat, still cradling Teddy in one arm while feeding him his bottle.

"You know, this is my very first time feeding a baby," he said softly with a smile.

I laughed and whispered back, "You know, this is my very first time hearing you speak in such a soft tone!"

"Very funny!" he whispered back.

"You're doing great, Lucky!" Amber said, "This is your first of many." And she turned on her heel and continued with what she had been preparing before Teddy woke.

CHAPTER 13
GUESTS ARRIVE

"Where is she? Where's my baby girl I let go to college?" Uncle Travis hollered playfully the minute he let himself in. And then in the next hefty breath, he announced, "Good Lord, it smells so darn good in this house. Is that Savannah's apple cake I smell?" he asked as he eyed her running down the stairs. He caught her and teased her, pretending that she was me. "Look what college has done to you—you've shrunk!"

Savannah giggled, "I'm not Dakota! I'm Savannah!" as if he were serious.

"Here I am!" I called three steps behind my niece.

"Well, that's more like it!"

Savannah said dreamily, still in Travis' loving hold, "Isn't that the most boot-i-full dress you've ever seen?" referring to mine. Cooper had left it on the front stoop last night for me to find this morning. It was boxed and wrapped with a big red ribbon. "It came from Cooper," Savannah continued. "All the way from Ing... land!"

"England," My uncle said. "I see." He gave me the once over—surveying the rhinestone spaghetti strap midnight blue dress that came to a hand above the knee. He gave a "hmmm" as his eyes looked disapprovingly at the length and hint of cleavage the dress allowed. "So, Cooper's back. I see. Will he be joining us today?"

"No. His brother is hosting Thanksgiving. Unfortunately, his daughter, Summer, is sick with a cold."

"Oh, that's too bad," he said. "Well, it was thoughtful of Cooper to bring you back such a pretty dress from the UK. Although an Irish sweater would have sufficed."

I laughed. I found my uncle's pretend naiveté adorable. "He told me he brought me back one of those, too!" I said excitedly. I knew better than to add, *I'm saving it for when he takes me to Rockport over Christmas break!* Texas didn't warrant wearing a heavy wool sweater, and although I loved my uncle immensely, he didn't need to know the romantic week Cooper had been planning for just the two of us. Cooper had told me visiting the quaint artist colony during winter was his favorite time to go. "*When the cold New England air whips at your face like a sunburn... but the serenity of being able to walk the beach without a soul around, is worth it,*" were his exact words. I had them memorized.

It was an evening I would never forget. We were lying on his bed, admiring the oil on canvas titled *Winter's Morning* after we had made love for the first time. He had bought the expensive painting for me, but I couldn't accept such an extravagant gift. So, he hung it in his bedroom and teased, "Well, you'll just have to come into *my* bedroom every time you want to admire it... Your painting that is."

I blushed, and he made love to me again.

"Hmmm," my uncle sighed as if he were reading my mind. For a moment, he looked hopeless, as if he had lost me, and told me with a slight pout, "I remember when you were this little," referring to Savannah as he balanced her on his hip effortlessly, and gave her another peck on her cheek.

She wasn't complaining about being held and pleading to be let down, as some kids do. Instead, she loved being held especially high. Travis was taller than her dad. I smiled and gave them a hearty squeeze as I told him how much I loved and missed him.

As we were headed into the den I mentioned, "He broke ground!" referring to the vacant lot Cooper purchased last year in Rockport to build a vacation bungalow.

"His ad agency is doing that well?" he asked. "That's outstanding!" he sincerely added.

"Yup—it's so exciting!" And then, before I could give details, Luke was walking toward us with Teddy, lightly tapping the infant's back, getting him to burp. Uncle Travis stepped behind him to look at the baby whose head was resting on Luke's shoulder.

"His eyes are wide open. So alert. That's a sign of intelligence, you know," Uncle Travis said, smiling, and added, "He looks just like you, Luke."

Luke smiled with that very proud, I-have-a-son grin. Then Teddy gave out a belch. "Good boy," Luke said, and then carefully placed him in his carrier and gingerly moved it to one of the large leather armchairs fit for a football player. All the furniture in the den was large and heavy-looking—very manly yet comfortable and of course made of good quality like everything else in the house.

"Cheap is expensive!" Amber Lee would say in retaliation when their American Express bill came in, and Luke would bark in damnation at the total! But his bark was always bigger than his bite, and within moments, the two of them would be cooing over something they both agreed on.

"What can I get you?" Luke asked, heading around the bar.

"Right now, I'll go for a beer."

"We've got bottled Stella, Amstel, Heineken, and of course Bud Light, but the Bud's in a can, so I've got to pour it in a glass. The Mrs. only allows cans for the pool patio."

"I'll take an Amstel."

I thought it was so sweet of Luke to oblige his wife's rules of etiquette. Our dad was the same way with my mom. Sometimes it freaked me out how similar the two men were, especially when Luke had never even met the man. I found it very commendable that Luke didn't show animosity towards his deceased mother, who kept such a secret. He simply had reasoned 'It is what it is'... and he always thanked 'the good Lord' he had me to make up for it. Even though we had different mothers, deeming us half-siblings, Luke never referred to me as his half-sister when introducing me to people, and I did likewise.

"Remember Betsy?" my uncle said with a giant grin.

Luke and I both nodded, remembering the voluptuous waitress from Rhonda's that my uncle had picked up during our dining there as a family and stayed until she got off work.

"We're an item now!" he said proudly.

Yeah, I'd say any man landing a relationship with someone more than half his age has something to be proud of—I guess. But I would admit, my uncle seemed very happy, and that's all that mattered to me, even though I would never date a guy twenty-plus years older than me.

Luke had fixed a Shirley Temple for Savannah, which she was merrily slurping through her spiral straw, recently given to her as a big sister gift. Most of the friends and family who sent Amber Lee and Luke presents for the new baby never forgot to put a little something in the package for Savannah. The drowned cherry was blocking the ginger ale from making it all the way to her mouth, causing a noise that reminded me of the suction straw at the dentist. Thankfully, she soon had enough and put her glass down, but took up swiveling back and forth on her round cushioned barstool, admiring her sparkly red shoes—tapping them together as if she were Dorothy.

All of a sudden, without warning, Lucky strode into the den as if he were on a catwalk. I nearly died. Lucky was dressed as Austin Powers! I thought my uncle was going to choke on his beer as Lucky shimmied. He roughly coughed as he eyed my new Asian, flamboyant, gay friend dressed in crimson velour bell-bottoms topped with a ruffled pirate-looking shirt. Around his open neckline hung a small yet identifiable Buddha charm in jade looped in a slender leather cord.

"You're Buddhist, too?" my uncle cried before even introducing himself, and I just wanted to crawl into a corner so ashamed of my uncle's rudeness.

But Lucky wasn't offended. He touched the charm, telling my uncle, "I can get you one. Onyx would be good for your skin tone—and Buddha symbolizes enlightenment and so much more." Then, suddenly, as if a brilliant idea popped into his head, he added with charisma and flair in a more assertive voice, "Even better, I know where *we* can get two large onyx horses for each side of your office entrance," gesturing with his arms the enormous size of the beasts.

Luke and I gave each other a look, anticipating what would come next out of my uncle's mouth. Nothing. He stood gaping. Good 'cause Lucky wasn't through!

With animated hands and a bold voice, Lucky continued, "The horse means power! It means strength, having will, determination, and a passion for freedom and justice!" Then he looked away from my uncle and stared ahead in mid-air as if he were reading a sign. The three of us looked in that direction, too. Lucky read his imaginary sign, pointing at each invisible word... "Perfect for The Law Offices Travis Kenwood." We all remained speechless... in awe. Lucky had a natural knack, a gift for capturing an audience.

A genuine smile came across my uncle's handsome face. Followed with his hand out to shake Lucky's. I was glad Lucky didn't attempt a hug. I inwardly laughed, knowing Lucky was in agony over my uncle's firm handhold!

Respectfully, my uncle added, "I'd like that very much, son. Thank you. And we'll go out for a cold one afterward!"

Son? Beer? Shopping? Holy moly! I couldn't believe it, and I couldn't believe Lucky remembered my uncle's name and referred to my uncle's practice to be "just," even with all the bad publicity it had received in the news media recently (that's probably how Lucky knew its name). I was grateful my uncle's initial reaction to my friend vanished. A wardrobe should have no bearing on what the person is like on the inside. My mom always followed the model "You catch more flies with honey!" and that was just what Lucky did beautifully. I smiled and pictured Mom in heaven smiling down on Lucky, too.

Within moments, Amber Lee and Luke entered the den and immediately admired my dress. "Dakota, where did you get that beautiful dress?"

Still standing, Lucky gestured to me and pirouetted me, and with just as much wonderment, he said, "You look absolutely stunning, my dear. Cooper has phenomenal taste!"

My uncle sighed and gestured to Luke for another beer. "Hold on to Savannah as long as you can," he said, "They grow up too fast."

He had no idea about what had happened to Savannah. Luke didn't think it was a good idea for him to know, and although I very rarely liked keeping secrets from my uncle, I wholeheartedly agreed with my brother's decision.

Just then, we heard jovial greetings as Savannah's grandfather, Drew, walked in with his longtime live-in housekeeper, Crystal. As my uncle had, they let themselves in too.

"Happy Thanksgiving!" Crystal cried as she ushered into the room and asked right away, "Where's that gorgeous baby?" and, as she narrowed in and found him asleep in his carrier, she expressed softly, "Oh, dear Lord, is he a vision." The woman hovered over Teddy like a moth around a light bulb.

Soon, more guests arrived—Crystal's daughter, Pamela, with her daughter, Alexis. No new boyfriend in sight. Alexis ran into her grandmother's open arms. After their embrace, Alexis climbed up onto a barstool and joined Savannah in spinning as if they were on the teacups in Disney World. Alexis was six months younger than Savannah and a year behind her in school. She lived about seven miles away, so sadly they wouldn't be going to the same elementary school. Drew joined Uncle Travis in a cold beer, and Pamela was already smitten with Lucky—captured in a conversation he had started. When the initial pageantry settled, Drew made his way over to Lucky, shook his hand, and told him it was a pleasure meeting him. He had a lot more couth than my uncle had initially, but sadly for me, I still saw Drew raising his eyebrows to Travis, mouthing, "Wow!" behind Lucky's back. I was disappointed, but I blamed this on their era—they weren't accustomed to people leading this lifestyle and seemed even more surprised with my bringing home someone who did!

I was glad my uncle and Pamela shared warm hugs and genuinely seemed sincere about each other's well-being. They'd almost made it to the one-year mark, which was big for my uncle, but his not wanting (more) children ended it. He liked Alexis and was nice to her even though she didn't reciprocate similar feelings towards him, but he didn't take it personally. She was just a meek child, unlike Savannah.

Teddy was beginning to wake, and Crystal was thrilled she could now hold him. Amber Lee offered if she'd like to go with her to change his diaper, and looking at Crystal's reaction, you'd think Amber Lee had given her a winning lottery ticket.

On their return from the makeshift changing area, Amber Lee had on the main floor in a nook that lay between the mudroom and the back stairs, Luke had prepared Crystal's gin martini with three Roquefort olives held together with the turkey toothpick.

Luke gestured, "In exchange for that baby you're holding!" as he sweetly retrieved his son from Crystal's loving hold.

With both hands holding her glass, she sipped her martini and admired the whimsical toothpick, "How adorable! Thank you, Luke, it's delicious."

"And for you, my dear," he said while handing Amber Lee a glass of white wine. She thanked him with a kiss on his lips.

Lucky was behind the bar fixing Pamela's Cosmo and, as he shook the vodka and cranberry juice cocktail looking like a pro, he asked, "I thought you were bringing the beau?" He poured the concoction into a chilled martini glass and squeezed a small lime wedge, and added, "Well?"

"Looks awesome. Thank you, Lucky." And after she took her first sip, she declared, "mmm… mmm… It's delish."

"Not the drink, dearie—your lover. That's way more interesting."

"Oh, he had to work." And before Lucky had a chance to ask what this guy did for a living, she said, "Don't ask. It's a long story… and he's not my lover."

Lucky and I got the hint she didn't want to talk about him, which was unusual for a new relationship. I pictured Mom waving a red flag!

As I was at the kitchen sink, washing the last of the delicate platters that weren't allowed in the dishwasher, I saw a shadow out the window.

"Lucky, someone's outside," I said, sounding startled.

"Maybe it's Cooper… surprising you again!" Then, as he walked over to the back door while drying a ceramic bowl, he saw the figure coming closer. "Oh, it's the other hottie—that detective!" he exclaimed.

"What's he doing here?" I muttered as I dried my hands and walked to the door just as Lucky was opening it, letting Detective Michaels in.

"Hi!" he said, "Hope I'm not coming at a bad time."

"Well, *it is* Thanksgiving," I said with wide eyes. I was expecting a quick apology followed by an explanation for his impromptu visit, especially since it was a major holiday.

But instead, he remained quiet, somewhat flustered, and there was a look about him reminding me of a schoolboy sent off to boarding school before his prime.

"Not to worry, we finished eating dinner," I said, and then offered, "You're welcome to stay for dessert."

"That'd be great!" he answered without hesitation. Then, turning back to the door, he told us with a bounce in his step, "I left something in the car. I'll be right back."

As soon as he was out of earshot, Lucky said, "Did you see that? One minute he's looking like *Oliver Twist* and then the next he's happy as a clam!"

I chuckled, "I know. Totally. Something I'd never expect from him."

"He has a crush on you."

"No. He. Does. Not!"

"Okay then. You have a crush on him!"

"I do not!" Then, eyeing his return, I quickly threw my dish towel at Lucky and ordered, "Quiet!"

As Lucky caught it, he announced, "All through—kitchen's clean!"

Detective Michaels came in carrying a manila envelope. For some reason, I thought it'd be a bakery box with sweets or a bottle of wine.

The look on Lucky's face made me think he thought so too, but he didn't question what was in the envelope. Instead, he said, "Let's go shoot some pool."

The men were already playing billiards. An NFL game was showing on the seventy-inch TV, Savannah and Alexis, I assumed, were in the playroom, and the three women were crouched together on the leather sofa looking through the first scrapbook/photo album of Teddy—twenty-five pages already filled, and he was only five weeks old! Crystal was ogling over the Halloween ones. Teddy was a peanut—literally, while big sis was an elephant.

"So precious!" she cooed.

"Hey, Shane!" Luke called, looking up from the billiard table after getting his shot, and before he aimed at his next solid, he came around the table to shake Detective Michaels' hand. "Good to see you, man."

Seconds passed before Drew and my uncle were doing the same and giving Detective Michaels friendly slaps on his back.

"Luke, you didn't tell me Detective Michaels was coming over," Uncle Travis said with a smile.

"Please, call me Shane," Detective Michaels said. "Luke wasn't expecting me. I apologize for interrupting, but I got some new info on the case that I wanted to share right away-it's good news."

Immediately, Luke was waving his hands like the guy who waves the planes out of the terminal, while my uncle was bending down behind the bar, looking for his special stock of bourbon.

In a matter of seconds, my uncle shot up, "Found it!"

Luke quickly came up with a plausible diversion as my uncle began pouring four shot glasses. "Nope. It's Thanksgiving. No business. Don't want to hear it. Tell me later, Shane. *Much* later." And was able to shoot him *the look* behind my uncle's view that blatantly read: *Shut Up, Shane!* As if it were written on his forehead with a Sharpie.

"What? There's more? What could possibly be good news? Jenning is dead already! He jumped off his balcony and that's the end of it!" Travis said all matter-of-factly and then looked over to Luke, who was beginning to look nervous—beads of sweat were trickling from his forehead.

"Luke, is there something you're not telling me?" my uncle asked, looking agitated.

When Luke didn't answer, my uncle was determined to understand why Detective Michaels was there. He spoke harshly, "If Dakota's in danger, I have a right to know, damn it!"

The ladies were startled and looked up.

I heard Detective Michaels curse under his breath as he combed his hands through his wavy hair. He had no idea Travis wasn't privy to any of Savannah's case. He must have assumed I had informed my uncle when clearly it was not up to me to do so.

I thought this was very unprofessional of Detective Michaels. It was a major holiday, not a workday, that he decided to pop in. This information was private, and the contents deeply personal. Didn't detectives take that same oath doctors and lawyers do with their patients and clients?

"Ladies, will you help me with dessert?" Amber Lee asked as she placed the ribbon bookmark and closed the album. Like her husband, she too looked nervous. I didn't blame her. What was about to implode wasn't good.

"Certainly," they both said. They were well aware of my uncle's temperament. Lucky scurried over to them and volunteered to carry the baby carrier. He followed the women with Teddy in tow, out of the room, to help set up the dessert table, make a pot of decaf coffee and tea, and whip the cream. I stayed behind. I wanted to hear what Detective Michaels had to say.

Before Detective Michaels divulged his "good news," Luke gave my uncle an abridged version of the incident with Savannah and her kindergarten teacher. I thought my uncle was going to throw his glass at the wall like Luke had when he heard about the crime, but instead, he chugged the liquor and slammed the glass down on the bar and refilled it. Luke began apologizing to him for not telling him sooner—explaining his reasons hurriedly and nervously. And suddenly I was the one who lost it!

"Enough! Lay off him! My brother had every right NOT to tell you! He's Savannah's father. Not you! And like you never told me about Alexis's dad being in jail because it wasn't something Pamela was proud of... the same rule applies to Luke. It's not something we want everyone to know." I could feel the tears welling up in my eyes, "It's not something we're proud of! We're... we're," I stuttered. "Stricken with guilt. We didn't see the signs," and just then, I was like Niagara Falls—the tears poured out of me as I cried, "Thank God, Savannah told me when she did."

It only took seconds before Detective Michaels came behind me and placed his hand on my shoulder to console me. And it only took a mere second for me to react. I elbowed him and pushed his hand off of me.

He stepped back, startled at my brusqueness.

I was practically shouting at Detective Michaels now, "And how could you? How could you come here on Thanksgiving and expect us to think any news from this case is good news? Nothing is good about this. Nothing! And how stupid of you to think that! And how stupid to assume my uncle knew. He's not even family!" And as soon as I spat those words: not family, I regretted it. As if it would make a difference, I blurted, "I mean, he's not blood-related to Luke!" I saw the hurt on my uncle's face, and before anyone had a chance to say anything, I flew out of the room sobbing...

How stupid of me... to imagine my uncle as anything less.

CHAPTER 14
CLOSING IN

I flew up the winding staircase to my room, slamming the door, collapsed onto my bed, and cried into my pillow.

Of course, Uncle Travis had to know how I looked up to him like a father. He and my dad had been childhood friends since the third grade. Their loyalty to one another bore just as strong a bond as blood brothers. Even though I was relieved that Savannah was not physically or emotionally harmed—unlike the other cases Detective Michaels shared with me that I wish he hadn't—I became easily defensive. Come to think of it, it was Detective Michaels who brought this anguish upon me that set off my nerves.

I replayed in my mind the tragic stories Detective Michaels told me in detail when we were at Willy's. We talked over my favorite snacks: nachos, buffalo wings, and potato skins.

And as he put back his third beer to my one Pepsi, he said, "Sometimes I hate my job." He explained how many unresolved cases there were of sexual abuse and how it turned his stomach when the parents denied it. "You can't imagine how many parents accuse their kids of lying." He had said, and then, with glossy eyes, he reminisced about one of the cases, "The poor girl finally had the courage to tell her mom she was being raped by her boyfriend—the mom's boyfriend that is— every time he slept over. And guess what mom's reaction was? She threw her out! This thirteen-year-old girl had gotten pregnant by that son of a bitch! After a DNA test revealed it was *his* baby, he was arrested. DSS stepped in. She's in foster care now… But it'll never be the same. Her childhood was robbed."

"And her heart was broken by her mom," I added.

I remember I had stopped eating and looked into his sorrowful eyes. He continued to tell me more—another case. When a stepbrother blackmailed his younger stepsister. He had threatened he'd tell her dad that he saw her steal money from his wallet unless she had sex with him, and how sex would be better than being locked in the shed for a weekend without food, water, or use of the bathroom.

"Please stop," I had said to Detective Michaels. "I don't want to hear anymore."

He ended with, "That son of a bitch convinced her they weren't related, so it wasn't all that perverse."

I imagined the girl squeezing her eyes shut as her stepbrother raped her.

My cell phone was going off. It was Cooper. I answered, "Oh, Cooper. It's terrible."

"What's wrong?"

"I said some really mean things."

"Who to?"

"Uncle Travis"

"What'd he do this time?"

"Detective Michaels showed up unannounced. He apparently had good news."

"What was it?"

"I don't know! I didn't give him a chance. Remember, Uncle Travis didn't know about Savannah, so Luke was trying to shut him up, but he didn't get the hint."

"So, what happened? How did your uncle take it? I can only imagine his temper got the best of him."

"He was pissed he wasn't told, but more hurt, I think, than angry."

"What the hell was Michaels doing showing up on Thanksgiving anyway? That's actually so rude. And I'm sure Travis was shocked. When you first told me, I wanted to pummel that pervert teacher! I'm sure your uncle's initial reaction to hearing this provoked similar feelings."

"You're probably right. And it was my fault for letting Michaels come in. Part of me felt sorry for him, thinking maybe he has no family. I don't know anything about his personal life. I invited him to stay for dessert."

"So, what exactly did you say that you think was mean?"

"After yelling at my uncle—defending Luke, I yelled at Michaels and basically called him unprofessional."

"That doesn't sound so bad," Cooper interrupted.

"Wait. In my rant, I blurted, 'Uncle Travis isn't family!' You should have seen the look on my uncle's face," I started to tear up.

"Dakota, your uncle totally understands what you meant. I know I do. What happened to Savannah is Luke's business. Detective Michaels should have known better than to assume Travis knew about it. Luke has only known Travis for, what, a little over a year? He isn't family to Luke. And to come over on Thanksgiving is wrong, just plain wrong, and to say he had good news. What could possibly be good news? You were angry about that and took it out on your uncle."

"That's exactly what I thought. God, I love you. You always understand what I mean. I just hope Uncle Travis sees it that way too."

"Dakota, just apologize. He'll never hold what you said against you. Geez, your uncle would do anything for you. Don't you know that?"

With a heavy sigh, I mumbled, "Yeah, you're probably right."

"I know I'm right, baby. Give your uncle time to digest this and remember, even though this was a terrible thing that happened to Savannah, it could have been so much worse, and thankfully, she is too young and naive and won't remember it."

"Yeah, you're right. I am just so exhausted, Cooper."

"I can imagine. Go to bed, baby. You'll feel better in the morning. This will all blow over soon. I promise."

"Oh, I hope so. I love you, Cooper. Thanks for always being there for me."

"My pleasure, baby. Love you, too. See you tomorrow. Bye"

It wasn't bedtime yet, although I desperately wished it were. I knew I had to head back downstairs. Savannah was counting on me. We'd worked as a team to serve the apple cake we made together for Thanksgiving. It was our tradition, and I wasn't about to let it go to pot. I combed my hair and retouched my makeup, and prayed that my uncle would forgive my irrationality.

When I entered the dining room, his seat was empty.

"Travis complained of an upset stomach and left," Drew said, and then added, "He's staying at Betsy's."

He was supposed to stay in our other guest room, adjacent to Lucky's.

I just shrugged and said, "Oh." As if it were no big deal, but inwardly I was thinking of something stupidly funny so I wouldn't make myself cry again. If there was one thing I hated about myself, it was my crying at the drop of a hat.

CHAPTER 15

TGIF!

Thank goodness it's Friday. Yesterday was the worst Thanksgiving ever. I slept in, which I usually did whenever I could. Lucky, however, was already in the home gym. He had scribbled on a Post-it and stuck it to the coffee maker.

In case you're looking for me, Buddha's belly's in the gym!

I walked in as he was uttering "Oy!" in between sit-ups, and my brother was hollering like a drill sergeant.

"Ten more!"

As I climbed up onto the seat of the stationary bike and began my own cardio workout, I hollered over the pop music, "You'll have a six-pack in no time, Lucky! Say bye-bye to Buddha's belly!"

Instantaneously, Lucky bellowed, "Yeah, baby!"

"One more set of ten, Lucky," Luke heaved in between his own set of fifteen, lifting twenty-pound weights with each arm. "And then speed walk on the treadmill for twenty minutes. Gradually, you'll move on to jogging."

"Oh, good. Can't wait!" Lucky retorted rather sarcastically.

"What? I'm surprised at you, Lucky. You're usually gung-ho about everything!"

"Just think," Luke chimed in, "your reward will be a hearty breakfast my wife's been preparing."

Lucky gasped in between breaths, "Okay, whatever you say, Luke!"

"Cooper's coming over tonight with his grandma and nephew, Charlie, for your special dinner," I said

"Summer's still sick?" Lucky asked.

"Unfortunately, yes," I pouted.

"Poor thing," Lucky said.

"I told him we'll wrap up a doggie bag for him to bring back to TJ and Linda."

"It'll be like takeout from Lucky's! It does have a nice ring to it." Then with slight hesitation, Lucky added, "Your uncle's coming, too—I hope."

I nodded, "I hope so." I knew I had to pull my uncle aside to apologize to him face-to-face.

"I hope he brings Betsy! I always make more than enough food."

"I don't know."

"Well, call him up and tell him he can," Lucky insisted. "You dial. I'll talk. Okay?"

Luke re-racked the dumbbells and then walked over to the bike and looked at me with sorrowful eyes, "Dakota, he knows you didn't mean it. It's me he's upset with. Besides, Travis is the last person in this world to ever hold a grudge against you. You're like a daughter to him."

"I'll apologize tonight. You can entertain Betsy, so I can have some alone time with him. Okay?"

"Okay," both men agreed simultaneously.

"Now what's his number?" Lucky asked as he slowed down the treadmill and picked up his cell phone, which was resting on the console.

"Don't think you're slowing down to talk on the phone counts as part of your twenty minutes," Luke said. "I'm keeping track."

I couldn't help but laugh, whereas Lucky rolled his eyes at me as soon as Luke turned away. I chuckled some more.

"I think I'm going to have to lie down when I put Teddy down for his morning nap," Amber Lee said after we all ate breakfast. "I didn't sleep very well last night."

As Luke stood up from the table, he kissed the top of her head, then called, "Come on, Lucky—to the stables!"

"Yay! Riding!" Savannah bellowed, "Yippee!"

"That's right! You're going to teach me how to ride Merry!" Lucky answered enthusiastically, "I can't wait!"

It was sweet, Lucky remembered the name of Savannah's pony. "It's a good thing you're riding today because tomorrow you'll be sore," I said.

Lucky looked at me quizzically.

I reminded him, "Your workout? There's a price to pay for just beginning to get in shape—especially the lightweights Luke had you do. Trust me—you'll be feeling achy tomorrow," I reiterated.

"But tomorrow we're going to Rhonda's! I'm going to ride the mechanical bull!" Lucky said, sounding disappointed as if this was the end-all. "I won't be able to ride it if I'm in pain."

"Oh, relax. My uncle has a solution—you'll see," I said, remembering how he coaxed Gloria's Pierre with shots of whiskey until the poor guy was begging to give it a whirl again. I laughed, remembering Gloria had told me bruises were mapping his rear end!

CHAPTER 16
THE APOLOGY

I lay on my bed reading. Everyone else was napping. Lucky's first real exercise workout, plus riding, tired him out, and it took less than fifteen minutes before he and Savannah were passed out on his bed with the beloved picture book, *Stellaluna*, resting across his chest. I gingerly took off his reading glasses and placed them and the book on the nightstand, and quietly left the room. I decided to rest too, but my type of resting was reading in a quiet atmosphere, and since everyone was napping, this was the ideal house of solace.

Uncle Travis arrived about two hours earlier than everyone else was expected to come over for dinner. I didn't hear him pull up.

I only knew he was present when he lightly tapped on my bedroom door and asked solemnly, "May I come in?"

"Come in," I answered.

"Move over," he said as he lay down on my bed next to me, resting his head on the adjoining pillow. We both stared up at my celestial ceiling, where I had adhered glow-in-the-dark planets and stars. "Which star is that?" he asked, pointing to it.

I also pointed to it while answering him, "That's the North Star."

He then took my hand and said, "Do you know what I think is the most prominent star?"

"I can guess."

"Go ahead then, guess," he said, giving my hand a quick squeeze.

"Me."

"How'd you know?"

"You always called me your star when I was little."

"As you ran into my arms," he reminisced.

"As I ran into your arms," I remembered fondly.

"And why is that?"

"Because I light up the room."

"And why is that?"

"Because I'm bright," I said, trying to hold back my tears.

"Why are you sad?"

"I let you down."

"Why else?"

"I let Savannah down."

"How?"

"I didn't protect her."

"Did your father protect you?"

"Huh?"

"Did your father protect you from being fatherless?"

"What?" I said, bewildered. "My dad didn't know he was going to die that day."

"The same way you didn't know Savannah's teacher was going to do what he did."

I let go. Tears streamed down my cheeks. "I'm sorry too for saying you weren't family. You know that's not true."

"I know you are, honey. Besides, you couldn't get rid of me even if you tried. Just like that song 'Wild Horses'... couldn't drag me away."

I laughed. "You know The Rolling Stones?"

"Of course. Mick and I go way back! But that's another story."

"Yeah, right," I rebutted, but then second-guessed it. "How do you know Mick Jagger?"

"Never mind. Now listen, Dakota. Life is like a tree."

I smiled, "Am I about to hear one of your inspirational lessons?"

He smiled. "Dakota, there are sturdy branches you can climb, but then there are those weak branches that make you fall, right down on your cute... what does Gloria call it?"

"Tuchus," I answered, laughing. It was good to be back to normal with my uncle.

"Yeah, that. Now, there are two things you can do after you fall: get up and either decide to never climb a tree again, never taking chances or challenges in life, *or* learn from your mistake and go at it again, but this time being careful by testing the branch out first, before putting all your weight on it. And you, being so young, have a whole forest of trees to choose from. There's no rush, so choose wisely and carefully."

"Okay," I said.

"Oh, and one more thing. Do you know who'll catch you *if* you do fall and who'll make you try again?"

"You."

"Do you know why?"

I sighed, "Because you love me."

"Yes, don't ever forget that. I also played outfield for *The Spartans* for six years," he joked, adding a little light humor into the mix. "Those nonsense words you spewed last night were like a giant fly ball waiting for me. I know you are distraught over what happened to Savannah. I am too. You also were very upset with Detective Michaels, and you let your emotions cloud your judgment of me... and that's all right. I forgive you, and I don't want you beating yourself up about it. Okay?"

I nodded and then plucked a Kleenex from my nightstand and blew my nose.

"Dakota, I may be ruthless when it comes to work, but when it comes to family—I'm worse than ruthless. I won't stop at anything before justice is served, and I understand my big mouth gets me into the media. And I understand Luke not wanting his daughter to be subjected to it and wanting to keep it private, so I'll let this not-telling-me slide, but I do want you to know—I have worked on and won many cases that never made the news. I *can* maintain a low profile. What disturbs me most is that you and your brother never gave me the opportunity. I have my quiet, yet poignant ways, too, you know. And I would make sure neither Savannah nor *any* child would ever be harmed by this."

"I'm sorry," I said, curling closer to him—nuzzling his chest like a giant teddy bear.

"I know you're sorry. That's why I'm here. I didn't want you crying at your Oriental friend's special dinner."

"Uncle—the PC term is Asian—not Oriental!" I said with a light slap to his chest, "and you sound like what happened to Savannah is viral. Do you know something you aren't telling me?"

"No. But after you stormed out, Michaels was left standing, looking most regretful that he stopped over. You know I wouldn't let him get away without explaining why he had come in the first place."

"Yeah, that, 'good news' he mentioned," I concurred, rolling my eyes, "how asinine he sounded."

"Yeah, the 'good news,'" my uncle repeated. "Dakota, I'm proud of you for telling Michaels off. He shouldn't have referred to it as good news—only news. It's up to the client to consider it good or not. I was surprised he didn't know that, but then again, he's young and still has a lot to learn."

"What was the news?"

"Another pedophile was arrested—linked to the photography teacher, and this low-life is willing to testify against him."

"Why? I mean, that's good, I guess, but I don't get it."

"Me neither. I've actually never dealt with sex crimes. Honestly, between you and me, I'd want to take the law into my own hands and castrate the…"

"I know, me too," I agreed.

"Good God, Dakota, I can't imagine someone raping a child."

"Savannah wasn't raped! He didn't lay a hand on her other than wiping ice cream off her face. That's how the whole thing started. That's how I found out! She told me when I was wiping Rhonda's barbecue sauce off her face, I was gentler than Mr. G."

"I know that—now. And thank the good Lord, Savannah is alright."

Suddenly, I didn't want to talk about it anymore. I wanted this weekend to be happy. I wanted to laugh with my uncle, not cry.

I patted my uncle's protruding belly and coaxed, "I bet Betsy would love it if you joined her in a Spin class."

"No way!"

"Cosmo said it's good for a couple's libido if they exercise together."

He chuckled, "Betsy reads that magazine too."

"Is she coming over for dinner?" I asked, hoping she was.

"Can't. She has to work. The weekend's the only time she can wait tables. She's in school during the week."

"Yeah? What's she studying?"

"Child psychology. She's got one semester left of her doctorate," he added, sounding proud, "Then she'll become Dr. Elizabeth O'Brian."

"Wow! I'm impressed. Doesn't come across as all that smart—no offense."

"None taken. I was surprised, too. But honestly, she is a smarty-pants, flirting the way she does—*only with* single male customers—to get higher tips—she told me so. She's paying for school herself."

"Wow. I had her pegged all wrong. Now I feel guilty. I thought she was younger, too."

"Younger?" he guffawed. "Younger than twenty-eight?"

"She looks like she's still in college?"

"She is!"

"You know what I mean—undergrad."

"Like you? Your age?"

"Not eighteen but a senior—twenty-two maybe."

"She makes me feel young," he said, smiling.

"Good, but regardless—you're still robbin' the cradle," I teased.

He chuckled, retook my hand, and pointed, "I love that picture of you," as he stared at the eight-by-ten framed photo of me eating ice cream. It leaned against the top shelf of my bookcase across my bed.

"Cooper does, too," I said, smiling.

"I remember when it was taken," my uncle said.

I rolled my eyes, thinking *Oh boy, another one of my uncle's embellished stories.*

"At Jennings'," he said, surprising the heck out of me.

"What? Are you sure?"

"Jake Senior always threw a Memorial Day barbecue. But after he died, his son nixed them… kept the Christmas party going, though. You were so proud you got your favorite flavored ice cream—strawberry. Before your mom wiped you clean, she took a photo of you because you looked so darn cute!"

"Oh. I don't remember that."

"Well, of course, you wouldn't remember it. You were only Savannah's age."

"How'd *you* get to go?"

"I did some legal work for the company. But after he died, Jake Junior went with another law firm, which turned out to be a blessing in disguise because I couldn't have represented you, suing Jennings Petroleum for your father's death. Weird how things turn around—huh?"

"Yeah, weird," I said, eyeing the photo, remembering how I told Cooper the correct flavor but hadn't remembered the rest.

Just then, Teddy began to wail.

"That baby!" Uncle Travis said all jolly-like. "Let's get him before he wakes everyone up, and give Amber Lee and Luke some more quiet time together... that's important, you know!"

I laughed, "Since when did you become a nanny?" As I followed him, knowing Teddy needed changing and like Lucky, I didn't think my uncle could decipher the front from the back of a diaper!

CHAPTER 17
SINGAPORE RICE NOODLES

Not only did Lucky prepare dinner, but he also set the table, and each place setting had a pair of wooden chopsticks he had brought with him. And, he also remembered to chill the case of Tiger brand beer he had purposely left behind in the trunk of my car. It was a nice addition to his special meal, and Luke was already on his second bottle. Like a child, Luke initially used them as drumsticks.

Tapping his plate with them, he jubilantly said, "Smells incredible—like a Chinese restaurant!" And just when Lucky lifted the tureen lid, revealing the main dish, Luke added, "Looks awesome, too!" and pointed to the floating bok choy with his chopstick, "Don't know what that is, but I'll give it a try!"

"Little boy," Amber Lee called playfully, looking at her husband, not five-year-old Charlie, who was sitting next to Savannah. The two of them were concentrating on getting their cherries out of their Shirley Temples. "Stop tapping!" Then, sounding motherly, she added, "You eat cabbage, so you'll like bok choy."

He immediately stopped tapping but still held them as if his plate were a drum and guffawed, "Jeez Louise, you're so worldly, baby!" Then he looked at everyone sitting around the table and practically announced, "I swear to god I married the smartest woman!"

"Luke, everyone knows bok choy!" I retorted.

"Travis, do you know bok choy?" Luke asked, hoping he didn't, so he could have a comrade.

"I actually do. Your dad and I would do Chinese Takeout every Sunday. Isn't that right, Dakota?"

I nodded, "Yup. And do you remember you and Dad had me make you boys Mai Tai's?"

"Oh, they did not!" Amber guffawed. Then she looked at my uncle, "Tell me she's joking?"

"What's the big deal?" he rebutted.

I laughed. "Yeah, and he'd end up passed out on the couch!"

"I don't believe my ears!" Amber Lee said, aghast with a hint of a smile, so I knew she really wasn't offended.

"Honestly, those were fun times, Amber Lee. After my mom died, my dad was very solemn. The more Uncle Travis came over, the more our house was full of laughter again."

My uncle smiled and gave me a wink. "Glad to hear that, darlin'. And really, Amber Lee—Tsk…Tsk for thinking I was a bad influence," he kidded, winking at her, too.

Cooper's grandmother, Jenny, asked, "Lucky, have you always liked to cook?"

And for a moment, I silently prayed the topic of cooking didn't lead to his mother's mysterious death, but I hoped Lucky knew better now and didn't want a repeat of the other night.

"Yes, ma'am," he answered, taking her plate and serving her first. Lucky had impeccable manners. Then eyeing her curved fingers, looking like rheumatism plagued them, he suggested, "Let me get you a fork and spoon. You can eat this like the Italians eat pasta!"

"Oh, that would be better. Thank you."

The buffet stood behind my chair. "I got it," I said as I opened the cutlery drawer and retrieved a fork, soup spoon, and knife, and placed them down next to her.

"I love rice noodles. Pile 'em high, pretty please," Jenny said cutesy-like.

"You got it!" Lucky said

"Your friend's lovely," she whispered to me as if it were a secret.

After Lucky had individually served each of us, Amber Lee recited the Lord's Prayer, and after we all said, "Amen," we dug into Lucky's scrumptious dinner.

CHAPTER 18
MECHANICAL BULL

Lucky wanted to sit with Savannah in the way, way back of the Volvo station wagon, looking out onto the incoming traffic. Luke drove, and Amber Lee sat up front, which left Teddy and me paired in the middle row. It only took about five minutes of the car moving before the baby was sound asleep again.

When we entered Rhonda's, the hostess seated us in Betsy's section. She had five other tables, but ours was the one she paid special attention to. Before we even gave our drink and appetizer orders, she arrived with them.

And when all was laid out, my uncle swooped her up in a sweet embrace and said, "Thank you."

She returned the smile, "You're welcome!"

Then he politely introduced her to Lucky, which thrilled me.

Before our entrées arrived, I made a beeline through the crowd to the ladies' room. When I came out of the toilet stall, I found Betsy at the sink washing her hands.

"Hey there, Dakota!" Betsy greeted me.

"Hi, Betsy! Congratulations, by the way."

"For what?"

"Your doctorate."

"Oh, that. Thanks, but I still have twenty more hours of lab work to put in for this one class before Professor Hard-Ass clears it… to earn my degree."

"Lab? Like you have to do some kind of experiment. Dissecting a brain?" I joked.

"Almost. I'm actually studying hypnosis."

"Hypnosis? Like hypnotizing people?"

"Yup," she giggled at my redundancy.

"Travis told me you want to be a child psychologist?"

"I do, and someday I hope to have my own practice. Oftentimes, a child who has been sexually abused keeps it a secret and only through hypnosis is it revealed—setting *it* free for the psychoanalysts to help the child cope and releasing any vital information for the criminal detectives to investigate."

I was completely taken aback and wondered if my uncle had told her about Savannah's case.

I interrupted, "Being able to accept any professional treatment is one step in the right direction."

"Yes. And to dislodge the belief that so many victims hold onto."

"That it was their fault," I interrupted.

Betsy nodded, "They suffer through their childhood into their adult lives, inwardly clinging onto this lie."

"Regardless of age, although the younger the better, there is still hope for a victim of sexual abuse to lead a normal and guilt-free life… right?"

"Of course. But instead of calling it normal, we like to refer to it as peaceful— a peaceful life. What's normal nowadays anyways?" Betsy said, drying her hands so thoroughly that the brown paper towel was beginning to rip.

"So, for your thesis, you are hypnotizing victims of sexual abuse?" I asked.

"Yes. And what's most difficult, believe it or not, is actually finding volunteers. Naturally, I need their consent. Most victims don't even know they're victims until something is triggered in their subconscious."

"Like what?" I asked, feeling enormously curious.

"I read a case where a new dad was bathing his five-year-old son, and suddenly a memory from his own childhood flashed in front of him when an older cousin babysitting him sodomized him in the shared bathtub, but it took him being a father for it to surface. Fortunately, in that particular case, the guy had an amazing wife who comforted him and encouraged him to seek counseling. She was understanding and didn't allow it to be brushed under the rug."

I remained speechless.

"There is hope for victims. But many resort to suicide before realizing this."

I immediately thought of Jake Jennings… He wrote how he was tired of pretending everything was normal when it clearly wasn't. Had he been a victim of sexual abuse?

"Dakota, are you okay?"

"Yeah," I quickly answered. "Sorry. So, it's hoping that made you want to become a child psychologist?"

"I guess you could say that. People ask me all the time why I would ever want to work with disturbed kids, and I usually shrug the question off and just say, 'I love kids!' But if there aren't adults who are hopeful for these child victims… they don't stand a chance."

Suddenly, the beeper attached to her apron was going off.

"Yikes! Gotta go! It's probably your table's food!" And she dashed out the door.

When I returned to our table, a Cosmo was waiting for me. I smiled and knew it was Luke who had ordered it for me. I fondly remembered the time he had poured a bucket of pool water over me to wake me up from my stupor after having had too many of those sweet cranberry and vodkas with Pamela at Drew's pool! Talk about making a bad first impression! But, being the incredible people they were, none of them judged me.

I carried the drink with me to the pen where Lucky was gearing up. The giant clock timer on the wall adjacent to the mechanical bull was set. We all gathered around as if it were some Olympic game we were watching.

Savannah was on Luke's shoulders, bellowing, "Go, Lucky! Go, Lucky!"

The Ding-Ding sound rang, and Lucky was off screaming, "Yee-haw!" as he had seen in the Westerns he had watched with his dear old granny.

CHAPTER 19
BACK AT SCHOOL

"Dakota, that was the best weekend of my entire life!" Lucky bellowed as he plopped down on my bed. "Can your family adopt me, please? And that Savannah of yours is like a little package from Tiffany's."

I smiled at the image of Savannah in a turquoise blue box, peering out like a nocturnal animal with the satin cream-colored bow atop her head.

"Savannah is a gift from God—isn't she?"

"Oh, honey, God broke the mold when he made her."

I smiled at his sweet words just as my cell phone rang. "Oh, great. It's Michaels," I said facetiously. "I can't deal right now."

"Let it go to voicemail."

"I'm going to."

"Dakota, as trite as it may sound, everything will work out. You can't stay mad at him forever, and deep down, you and I both know he meant well. You know, I didn't want to say anything—after all the bullshit that went down that evening, but did you ever find out what he had in the manila envelope?"

"My uncle told me it was evidence of another pedophile linked to the photography teacher."

"Well, I suppose that is good news... just bad timing—delivering it that is," Lucky said, pulling himself up off my bed. "I've gotta go get some shuteye." As he kissed me and wished me goodnight, "*Bonsoir, mon amie.*"

I lay in bed trying to fall asleep, wishing Jezebel would walk through the door at any moment. She had phoned earlier to let me know her flight was delayed and didn't want me to worry. She was an awesome roommate and very considerate. I couldn't get what Lucky had said earlier, about Detective Michaels meaning well, out of my head. I reached for my cell phone resting on my nightstand and scrolled down to Hottie Detective without even listening to the message he had left two hours earlier. He answered on the first ring.

"Dakota?"

"Yeah, it's me," I said.

"So?"

"So… what?"

"Didn't you get my message?"

"I haven't bothered to play it—I'm calling back instead," I answered and desperately wished I had played his message before calling him. I could tell in his voice that something was wrong.

"That's not a good habit, Dakota," he reprimanded. "We need to meet," he spoke firmly.

"Detective Michaels, I don't think I want to know any more about the investigation."

He remained quiet as if waiting for me to explain why.

"It's very upsetting to me. I need to concentrate on my studies. Rice isn't easy, you know? Savannah is all right, and I just want to move on." Surprisingly, he didn't interrupt. "Since this has all started, I've been on edge and I've gotten into arguments, making verbal accusations that have hurt the people I love the most, and it's just not worth it."

There was a long pause.

"Detective Michaels, are you still there?"

"Yes."

"Why do we have to meet?"

He didn't answer.

"God... you're really getting on my nerves." I gave in, "Just tell me now."

"I'd rather tell you in person than over the phone." Then, with a heavy sigh, he added, "Dakota, I need to show you something."

"Fine. Come over," I caved.

"I'm leaving now."

And click, he was gone—heading to my dorm. I could feel myself becoming a nervous wreck. I told myself to calm down. It was the longest fifteen minutes of my life! And as I waited, I decided to play the voicemail.

The front desk called to let me know I had a visitor. I pulled on a sweatshirt over my pajama tank top and headed downstairs to sign him in.

We didn't greet each other as we had in the past. No quick peck on the cheek from me or a warm one-armed hug from him. He had a manila envelope in one hand. The moment we entered my room, I told him to take a seat. He pulled out my desk chair, and I sat on the desk.

I crossed my legs, leaned against the wall, stared at him, and asked, "So what is it?"

He took a deep breath. "After you stormed out of the room the other night, your sister-in-law was kind enough to walk me to the front door.

"You mean when you rudely interrupted our Thanksgiving?"

"Dakota, I apologize. I regret my impulsiveness."

I shrugged, "Okay... go on."

"Your niece, Savannah, came down the stairs with her friend, Alexis."

"Yeah."

"Did your uncle or brother tell you why I came over that night?"

"You mean did they tell me your *good news?*" I returned, agitated.

He ignored my behavior. "Well, did they?" he asked flatly.

"Yes. My uncle told me you told him another pedophile was caught, linked to this case, and is willing to testify against the photography teacher."

"The pedophile's home was searched..." he paused.

"And?"

He looked pensive.

"Will you just tell me already? What did you find?" I was annoyed with his prolonging the news.

He began opening the envelope and started pulling out what looked like a dozen eight-by-ten photographs, but stopped. "Dakota, this pervert had a ton of photographs... nude pictures of children displayed as if they were decorations. He even cut some out and made a collage on the bedroom wall across his bed. Sick bastard."

I began to feel perspiration forming on the insides of my palms. I wiped my sweaty hands on my thighs and nervously whispered, "Were any of them Savannah?"

He didn't answer me right away and continued to describe the photographs. "Different poses. Some look as if the girls didn't know their picture was being taken. We don't know any of their names."

"Okay, so none of them were Savannah because you know her." I felt a slight relief. "But then why are you here?"

There was something at once calm and deadly in the way he spoke. "At the precinct, they are referred to as Red Bow—what she wore in her hair. White Bunny—the stuffed animal she was holding. Pink Tutu... you get the point, Dakota."

"What are you getting at?"

"But after that night—Thanksgiving, I can match these photographs with a name. These photos of the same girl," he said slowly, taking out the photographs and handing them to me.

"Oh, my God!" I cried, "Alexis." I flipped through the photos, and a sudden pang hit my stomach as if someone had punched me in the gut. The photos dropped to the floor, and I ran to the bathroom, knelt by the toilet, and hurled.

Minutes passed before I lifted myself off the floor, stepped to the sink, and turned on the faucet. I looked into the mirror and stared at my burning eyes. I watched the running water clean away my mouthwash, the basin white again, and I thought how great life would be if terrible stuff could easily be washed away, and forgotten.

Detective Michaels was still sitting, waiting for me.

I stepped out of the bathroom, wiping my hands dry on a towel, "This explains her timidness. There was always a tenseness about her posture when she was around Hubbell, Cooper, Uncle Travis... even Luke, which I thought was unusual considering Luke wasn't a stranger."

Michaels did not comment. It was as if he wanted me to air my suspicions.

"I had brushed it off, excusing her meekness, thinking it was due to her being raised by a single mother while her dad was in prison for drug smuggling." That inevitable question: *What if...* loomed inside of her, but despite their broken marriage and his being sent to prison, what had kept her going was her baby. Alexis was the center of her world. And this new evidence was going to crush her.

"What are you thinking, Dakota?"

"I feel terrible for Alexis, but even worse for Pamela. This is going to kill her."

Detective Michaels nodded.

"She's going to blame herself... and fear her ex-husband will get custody," I cried, plopping down on my bed. "You know he's out and on probation-right?"

"Dakota, I highly doubt he'll get custody," Michaels answered as he walked over and sat next to where I lay... close to my side. He looked at me for a second as if I were a math problem he was trying to figure out. Then he held my hand and apologized. We both knew this wasn't his fault, but I suppose those words: *I'm sorry*, were the only words that fit at that moment. The universal words that come out of a person's mouth during desperate times, and this being one of those, *I'm sorry* sounded best.

Michaels stood and stepped to the mini-fridge, opened it, and retrieved two bottles of water. He handed one to me. I sat up and thanked him.

Then he asked, "Dakota, what did you think of Jake Jennings's suicide note?"

"What?" I choked on the gulp of water I just took. Still coughing, I managed, "What does *Jennings* have to do with this?"

Michaels was quiet.

I remembered my uncle had initially told me there wasn't a suicide note, and how it took Savannah using the blank side of it to draw a picture for me to find out the truth. She had spotted his open, disorganized briefcase in our kitchen and grabbed the first loose paper. When I confronted him with it, he had a plausible excuse and told me he had not been privy to it until that day, and he was waiting for the right moment to tell me. He seemed genuine, and I believed him.

"Dakota. What's wrong?"

"I had a gut feeling there was one the whole time. I was glad when the detectives finally found it."

Michaels looked grave, "Jennings didn't *leave* it... he had mailed it to your uncle."

"What?"

"He planned his suicide. Most do."

"I'm so confused. Why didn't he just leave the note in his penthouse? Why'd he mail it to my uncle?"

"Did you read it?"

"I took it from Savannah's little hands in shock... the look on my face scared her because she began to cry and asked why I didn't like her picture."

Now, Michaels was the one who was shocked, "What?"

"What do you mean, what?"

"That means your uncle didn't show the police the letter until *after* you found it."

"You're losing me here."

"When we saw the note, it had that drawing on the backside! He played it off that he knew nothing of the picture."

"Why would he do that?"

"He was holding back evidence. Dakota—that's breaking the law."

"Why would he hide it? I'm so confused."

"That explains it," Michaels said as if a light bulb just went off in his head.

"Explains what? Michaels, please tell me," I pleaded.

"There was more to Jennings' suicide letter."

"What do you mean?"

"We asked to see the envelope that the letter came in, and it wasn't a business-sized envelope but a large manila eight-by-ten-sized envelope."

"Like the one you brought over?"

"Yeah... like the one I brought over," he repeated. Then, in a daze, he said, "That son of a bitch."

"Who?"

Forgetting for a split second, I adored my uncle, Michaels angrily blurted, "Travis! God damn it! He's hiding something!"

I was speechless.

Michaels recollected, "Travis saw the surprised look on the lead investigator's face of the sized envelope Jennings used for a *paged letter* and defended, 'I guess Jennings didn't want to fold his letter.' But *I* noticed the stamps."

"What?"

"Dakota, Jennings had put a lot of stamps on it… too many in fact, and when your uncle saw the look on *my* face, he remarked, '… and wanted to make sure it got to me!' and laughed it off like it was no big deal. But like you had a gut feeling about the missing suicide note, I had a gut feeling there was more in that envelope than that suicide note."

"Oh, my God. Why? What's there to hide?"

"That explains it." .

"Explains what? What does it explain?" I repeated, nervously.

"Dakota, what did you think Jennings meant when he wrote how he still struggles—seeing his 'five-year-old self as a victim?'"

"I don't know… I don't know," I cried, "You tell me! What did he mean?"

"Dakota, that's what I'm trying to find out. I think your uncle's hiding more evidence." Then, as quickly as Detective Michaels came over, he fled. "I've gotta go, Dakota!" And just like that, he was out the door.

I didn't waste any time either. I called my uncle. It went to voicemail. I left an urgent message but made sure not to sound like I was livid with him. I acted as though I was desperately sad, knowing very well that it would grab his attention.

"If you're still at Betsy's and not already halfway home to Fort Worth, can you please swing by here as soon as possible? It's midnight now. Jezebel won't be back till tomorrow, and I really need you. Please," I begged.

Within seconds, he phoned back. He sounded out of breath. "Dakota, is everything all right?"

"Sorry for bothering you guys."

"Dakota, you're more important," he said with the utmost sincerity, but I wanted to shout: *Oh, really? Then why'd you lie to me?* But instead, I remained quiet, allowing him to ask, "What's wrong, Dakota?"

"Can you put Betsy on?"

"Why?"

"Please."

I had assumed correctly—she was right next to him. "Dakota, what's up?" Betsy asked, cool as a cucumber.

"Has my uncle had a few too many?"

"Yeah, but why?"

"I'll come there then," Not giving her a chance to refuse, I asked, "What's your address?"

She obliged.

"See you soon," I said.

"Okay," she returned, sounding weary.

I clicked off and grabbed my car keys, and headed out the door. What I was about to do needed to be done face-to-face.

CHAPTER 20
AT BETSY'S

GPS said my destination was twenty-three minutes away, but I made it to Betsy's in eighteen. She rented the bottom floor of a two-family house with two other roommates who weren't back yet from visiting their families out of state for the holiday, which was great because that meant I could have it out with my uncle! As soon as I stepped up onto the front porch, I could hear a television blaring, and before I had the chance to ring the doorbell, Betsy opened the door. She must have seen my car's headlights.

"Hi!" she greeted and instantly apologized. "The upstairs tenant–aka my very old, hard-of-hearing landlord, always falls asleep with the TV on."

"Oh, that would drive me nuts!" I said.

"Us too, but he hasn't raised our rent in five years, so we keep our mouths shut. We just keep a surplus of these bad boys to help us," and she reached for a mason jar full of neon orange foamy things a little larger than jelly beans. "Earplugs," she said, "my roommate gets them for free—she works with heavy machinery that's so loud she says she can't even hear herself think."

Just then, Uncle Travis headed out of the bathroom wearing his burgundy, terrycloth robe, "Dakota darlin', what's wrong?"

"I'll give you some privacy," Betsy said. "Make yourself at home, Dakota," as she pointed to the living room for me to sit. "Can I get you something to eat or drink?" she asked. "It won't be any trouble."

She was so sweet.

"No, thank you. Well, maybe some water, please," I said.

"You got it!" As she brushed past my uncle, he stopped her and said with an endearing smile, "Thank you."

Uncle Travis took a seat across from me in the La-Z-Boy but didn't recline the chair to put his feet up. Instead, he sat at the edge of it.

Betsy returned with two glasses of water, placing my uncle's beside him on the table, and handed mine to me, smiling, "Here you go, Dakota. Okay then, I'm off to bed."

And mere seconds before her hands grabbed a pair of earplugs, I asked, "Betsy, would you mind staying up?"

She looked at me with furrowed brows.

"Dakota, what's this about?" my uncle asked with matched confusion.

"Dakota, I would rather not get in the middle of any family squabble," Betsy answered.

"I may need your help," I replied, "your expertise in psychology."

Now my uncle was giving that proverbial deer-caught-in-headlights look

"You lied to me... about Jennings' letter."

"Dakota, I told you already—I had found out about it that day… when Savannah used it to color on."

"You left out the part where it came in the mail… to your house!"

He looked as if he were an amateur magician trying to pull the rabbit from his hat, but couldn't manage.

"Tell me!" I cried.

"Dakota, what's the big deal?"

"Michaels told me the envelope it came in was large with a lot of stamps on it!"

"So?"

"So, there was more to it!"

"Not necessarily. And besides, what Michaels *thinks* has no bearing."

"Don't even go there! It may work for you in the courtroom, but not here. Not now!"

"Help me out," he said, looking at Betsy, who was looking dumbfounded—I'm guessing she was surprised at my talking back to my uncle and shocked by his keeping such secrets.

She said calmly, "Travis, aren't you obligated—sworn to the oath—to declare all evidence?"

For once, my uncle was speechless.

"The man tried to kill her. If there was more to his letter, I don't know why you wouldn't want Dakota to know that. She needs closure."

"You don't understand," he said. Then, sitting back down, he put both his hands over his face. Seconds later, we could hear, "Oh God. Dear God." Something I had never seen him do before.

Of course, he cried at my mother's funeral, but he stood stoically as a few tears streamed down his cheeks, remaining in charge as if my father and I depended on his strength to pull us through the days of her wake and funeral. And when my father died, he acted in the same manner but stronger. He took charge of all the arrangements. He took control of everything, and I was forever grateful. I couldn't do it alone. I was sixteen at the time and on the verge of a nervous breakdown. But here he was—two years later in the home of his lover, teary-eyed. I could sense he knew something terrible and was desperately trying to keep it from me.

"What else did Jennings confess to you with this letter?" Betsy asked. "Dakota has a right to know," she said, sounding strong, unwavering like a professional psychologist.

"Betsy, I need to talk to you privately," my uncle was able to say in between heavy breathing.

"Like hell you do!" I shouted. "Enough! Enough secrets!" Then I began to cry, "You used to tell me everything."

"Dakota, this is something you don't need to know."

"Why?"

"It will ruin you."

"How?"

"It's something you don't know. Something you forgot about. You were just a baby."

"How old, Travis?" Betsy asked, sounding as if she just figured out what this terrible thing was.

"Four and then... " he stopped himself.

"Four and what, Travis? This is way more crucial than you think," she demanded.

He mumbled, "Seven."

"Seven?" I repeated, making sure I heard him correctly.

He nodded.

"What's the significance of age seven?" Betsy asked.

"My mother was diagnosed with cancer, and they were keeping it a secret from me," I answered.

"Oh. I'm sorry," she said with a worried frown.

"Dakota, please trust me. I know what's best. You don't need to know what was with the letter," my uncle pleaded.

Uncle Travis took multiple sips of his water. Then looked at Betsy, "You got anything stronger?"

She shook no, although I highly doubted there wasn't a bottle of booze around. "I might be able to scrounge something up after you spill the beans," she said, looking at him with her arms crossed. I was beginning to really appreciate her candor.

Then he looked up at her with solemn eyes and tenderly spoke in a hushed voice, "I wish it were just spilled beans, dear. It's something far worse, Betsy. Something I'm sure you have studied and perhaps something you may have experienced yourself." Then he stood up from his chair and walked over to me on the couch and sat beside me. Betsy looked utterly shocked. Now she was sitting on the adjacent recliner with her face in her hands.

"Dakota, there was an additional letter made out to you."

Both Betsy and I gasped in unison.

"It was an apology letter."

"So, he rigged the pipe," I cried, "killing my dad?"

"No."

"Then what?"

"Jake Jennings apologized for his father's actions," my uncle finally confessed.

Instantly, remembering the night Jake Jennings broke into my home, I blurted, "Jennings told me that his father was evil! He told me how much he loathed him, saying, 'he made me do it. ' Telling me over and over again, 'he made me do it, Dakota, but I didn't know what he was talking about. Then I asked him, 'he made you smuggle drugs?' but I knew his dad died before he became involved with the Colombian cartel—Pamela had told me so."

Betsy interjected, reminding me, "He said he was apologizing for *his* dad. What *his* dad did. And *his* dad wasn't alive when *your* dad died," emphasizing the pronouns way too much—my head was beginning to pound.

It was as if my uncle didn't hear a word we said. He was shaking his head, repeating, "Dear Lord… Dear Lord."

"Uncle Travis," I pleaded, "Please explain what he was talking about."

"You were too young to remember. I didn't want his note to bring back something you never knew happened to you," he said.

"You're doing it again. You're skirting the whole truth," I replied with tears streaming down my cheeks. In actuality, I *was* fearful of the truth.

Trying to sound composed, my uncle confessed. "You are an adult in the eyes of the law. But you are a child in my eyes, Dakota… an innocent child," his voice was beginning to crack again. "You are giving me no choice. You are forcing me to tell you, and I hate that, Dakota. If there is one thing I hate most in this world, it is doing something I feel wholeheartedly will not make the outcome better… only worsen the future and your beautiful mind."

"How terrible can it be?"

"Jennings was forced to take pictures of you. Photos his dad treasured."

"Go on," Betsy encouraged.

My uncle looked up at her with disapproving eyes. He was shaking his head and looked as if he wanted to summon her to her room.

"She's going to remember it sometime in her life, Travis," Betsy began to raise her voice, "Better she gets help now than later. She has her whole life ahead of her. What happens when she's married and has a kid, and all of a sudden a nice moment with her own child vividly brings back a similar moment she experienced as a child that began as sweet and innocent, and now as an adult she remembers what Jennings really did to her that is far from innocent?"

"She's right," I said calmly. "Please tell me what happened to me when I was seven."

"Jennings senior was fond of your parents. He seemed like a genuine guy. When he found out your mom had cancer, he showed up with flowers and insisted that if there was anything he could do to help in any way, not to hesitate. He especially spoiled you and sweet-talked your mom, telling her how lucky she was to have such a beautiful little girl and how he wished he and the Mrs. could have had another child, but were blessed with a wonderful son, and when his wife died, he said it made him miss a female presence all the more. He always joked about how a female's laughter was like a sweet melody that made a house a home, and how Dakota's giggle was that sweet melody he so dearly missed. Hell, Dakota, he even had me fooled. So, the times when your dad had to spend all day with your mom at the hospital when she was having chemotherapy, and I was too busy at work, my secretary picked you up from school and dropped you off at Mr. Jennings. You seemed excited to go. He had a pool and trampoline… and puppies!"

"Puppies?" Betsy chimed in, sounding disgusted.

I waited patiently, feeling nervous about the outcome, and for a moment I wondered if this was how my mother felt when she was at the doctors' awaiting her test results. How terrible she must have felt. And how horrified and guilty she would feel if she were alive today, not having detected the true Mr. Jennings Senior. I imagined her praying right now. Praying what had happened to me when I was seven wouldn't kill me now, eleven years later.

"Oh, how you loved it when his German shepherd had a litter. Even when your parents weren't at the hospital, you begged them to take you over to Jennings' home. You were there practically every day! You said you were helping the mommy dog take care of her babies so she could nap. It was so adorable. You were so adorable. He even let you name them. There were four, and you named them, Eeney, Meeney, Miney, Moe!"

Lucky's lesson behind that rhyme surfaced as I shook my head, "Why didn't he give me one?" I asked.

"He wanted to, but your mother's oncologist didn't think it was a good idea because of her low immune system, and an allergy would make it worse."

"She wasn't allergic to Buddy, our cat."

"That tabby was more outside than inside. Remember when he dropped his kill on the front stoop as if to say: here's dinner! What was it—a chipmunk, bird?"

I shrugged my shoulders

"Oh, but how your mama tried to convince Jethro that she'd be all right if you got a puppy, but your dad didn't want to take any chances. He told her, 'Dakota can survive without a puppy, but we cannot survive without you, Loretta.' And that was the end of your- getting-a-puppy conversation."

I finally succumbed to the inevitable, "What did Mr. Jennings do to me when I was seven?"

He hesitated. Buried his hands in his face. I felt like I was on a raft out at sea, and the air was slowly escaping through a tiny, pierced hole. I could hear it whistling out as my weight was pushing against it.

He revealed his teary face and spoke softly, "He played with you... sexually, Dakota, while his son took pictures."

I wanted to drown. Shrink. Hide. Become invisible. I was numb. I felt cold. Freezing cold. Tears sailed down my cheeks in one quick stream.

Uncle Travis placed an afghan over me and whimpered, "I'm sorry. I'm sorry, Dakota. I'm so sorry."

I couldn't speak. Exhaustion and grief inched heavily into every fiber of my body. My mind flickered as if on a short circuit, spitting never-ending images of anxiety, anguish, and sorrow at me.

My uncle's whispers, "I'm so sorry," became monotonous.

I nodded—the only response I could muster. The aching sadness grew inside me like poison in a witch's cauldron. It was something indefinable I'd already been living with for months since finding out what had happened to Savannah... and now, enflamed by Jake's suicide letter, and its cryptic message... revealing what had happened *to me* made the intangibility so much worse. I curled myself in the fetal position on Betsy's sofa, closed my eyes, and fell asleep.

CHAPTER 21
THE MORNING AFTER

When I opened my eyes in the sunlit room, my uncle Travis was standing in the vestibule staring at me, waiting. He was dressed in his velour, navy-blue jogging suit. He had once told me it was what he wore on long drives because it was ultra-comfy. And if it were a business trip, he made sure he allotted enough time to change into one of his custom-tailored three-piece suits.

I quietly asked, "Who is it this time?"

"What?"

"Where are you going and who is it you're saving or putting away?" I asked, assuming he was headed to one of Texas' metropolitan areas and either defending or prosecuting some millionaire extortionist.

"Nowhere. I'm staying with you today… and tomorrow and the next. However long it takes, Dakota."

Then at that precise moment, Betsy called from the kitchen, "Breakfast is ready!"

I slowly got up. My head was pounding. I had a major migraine. I felt dizzy and fell back down onto the sofa. Uncle Travis rushed over to me. He sat beside me and rubbed my back.

"I'm so sorry, Dakota. I wish I could take away your pain." Then he slowly kissed the top of my head and suggested, "Maybe something to eat will help… a little."

I nodded in agreement, but first told him I had to use the bathroom. He walked me to it, letting me lean on him as if I were an old lady. It reminded me of my grandma when I helped her to the john in the middle of the night. She always felt bad for waking me up. It was almost comical how clueless she was about how much noise she made. I remembered chuckling as I made my way to assist her; putting on her slippers, and her bathrobe, turning on the light, and refilling her glass of water—all before going tinkle, as if she were the only one in the house! My parents never complained to her. They used to say that the toughest job was raising a happy and healthy family, and the second toughest job was taking care of elderly parents.

Betsy piled cheesy scrambled eggs, two sausage patties, and a slice of whole-wheat toast onto my plate.

Uncle Travis said stoically, "We'll get through this, Dakota. I promise. Whatever it takes. Okay? You know I'm here for you… always." And took my hand.

I gripped it, feeling relieved for a moment that Michaels never saw the photos of me. I could only imagine what mine would be referred to as, down at the precinct: the girl with ice cream, a girl with puppies. *Did Mr. Jennings pose me with his puppies?* I imagined myself naked with the puppies lapping at the dripped ice cream. The thought of something so innocent and sweet turning ugly made me nauseous.

"I want to see the photos," escaped my mouth.

My uncle took his time responding. But slowly began. "A manila envelope without a return address was in my pile of mail. I hadn't gotten to my mail in over a week, but I noticed its postmark was two days before his death. My housekeeper had my mail piled in stacks on the kitchen island according to size. She had put this envelope with the magazine issues, and as I flipped through them, I spotted this bulky envelope. He had even enclosed the negatives—he used an old camera. And scribbled on a note were the words: *developed myself.* I remember Jake as a boy interested in photography and his dad having a dark room built in their basement for him to learn how to develop film. At the time, I thought his father was a great guy, helping his son pursue a hobby. I hadn't a clue what sickos the Jennings men were."

I mumbled, "What's going to happen to them?"

"Only the three of us sitting in this room know about the photos."

"They'll find out."

"Dakota, I think the cops want closure, too. They're probably content with the idea that Jake was apologizing for his acting violently towards you, and not having the equipment checked, causing your father's death and leaving you orphaned." Then he inappropriately chuckled, "Makes for a great story."

"Yeah, but he mentioned his dad, who's been long gone before any of that started."

"Regardless, Jake was a criminal! And dead! The cops are probably ecstatic they can put this case to rest."

"Yeah. I suppose you're right."

"I know I'm right," he said, in a fatherly tone.

"So where are they?" I asked.

"What? The photos?"

"No. Your magazines!"

"Dakota Summer Buchannan, don't get fresh with me! As far as I'm concerned, they are mine. They were mailed to me... becoming my property. Possession is nine-tenths of the law."

I stayed quiet. I hated when he spoke law with me.

"What do you think I did with them?" he asked calmly.

"Burned them?" I answered.

He nodded, "You know me well. That night, I had the biggest bonfire—accompanied by a bottle of Wild Turkey. "I didn't want one trace of those photos around."

Betsy spoke, "He did the right thing by burning them. You don't need to see them. It would only make it worse." Then, after refilling all our coffee mugs, she explained, "Visuals stimulate the brain—making the unbelievable—believable. But now that you know what was done to you, you can get help if you feel it has affected you, but if you don't remember any of it—if you haven't experienced nightmares or visions of Mr. Jennings touching you..." She placed a warm hand on my shoulder, "then you'll be alright. The photographs would have only brought something to life that you never knew existed. The images would have planted themselves in your psyche, and you would have second-guessed yourself. You could have started having visions and nightmares of the photos, not of the actual experiences." Betsy paused before finally asking, "Do you understand? Am I making any sense to you?"

"I do understand. It reminds me of the Holocaust."

"O...kay," she said slowly, sounding puzzled. "How so?"

"General Dwight D. Eisenhower provided cameras for every American soldier overseas to take pictures of what they saw when they liberated the Jews from the concentration camps because he thought no one would ever believe such an atrocity unless they saw it. Millions of black and white photographs illustrate the Holocaust for those too ignorant to believe what is written. Eisenhower was a brilliant man."

"You do understand," she said, sounding relieved.

"I also read in some science magazines that children's memories of childhood are triggered more by photographs in the family album and constant reminders by their parents than by actually remembering the event. Their brains just aren't large enough to store it all because it's too busy growing."

"Yes. That's also true," Betsy agreed.

"Do you think if you believe something hard enough, it will happen?"

"Or not happen?" Betsy added.

"What do you mean?" Uncle Travis asked, looking concerned. It was almost like Betsy and I were getting too analytical for him, even though he was an intuitive and bright lawyer.

"You believed I would forget what he did," I rephrased.

"Yes. And you *had* forgotten," he said simply. "You're normal!"

"Normal is so vague," Betsy scolded.

"Would you have believed me if I had a flashback and confided in you?" I asked.

"You never were one to make up tales. Besides, this is something too obscene for any child to imagine. I would have believed you, Dakota."

"I'm glad you said that, Travis." Betsy's face was empty of expression. "So many parents don't believe their child. Oftentimes, persons who have been sexually abused keep it hidden because they are so ashamed, and believe revealing it to anyone, a parent, friend, or trustworthy adult, is hopeless." Betsy paused a moment before she finalized her thoughts, "Dakota, Jake Jennings may have been sexually abused by his father, and that may be the reason why he killed himself."

"His autopsy report revealed he was a coke addict," my uncle informed me.

"His suicide note mentioned it," I reminded him.

"Most sexual abuse victims depend on alcohol or narcotics to mask the pain," Betsy added.

"And his involvement with the Colombian cartel probably was more forced upon them—they needed a safe exit out of the airports more than he needed the lucrative money," my uncle replied.

The two of them nodded in agreement as my head was spinning—this all sounded like a scene from Law and Order. My heart felt as if it were crumbling up inside of me like a burning piece of paper. I was numb and mute. Everything registered, but I couldn't move.

"I still don't feel sorry for the bastard," my uncle said coldly.

I wanted to say, *Me neither*, but couldn't. An ounce of me felt sorry for Jake Jennings. He made the right decision—confessing the wrongful deed he did, but should that give him immunity and a ticket into heaven? Had he taken away my innocence blindly? An ounce of me was grateful for his not sending me the photos.

Perhaps Jake Jennings thought if I ever "re-countered the trauma" as Betsy put it, sometime in my adult life and couldn't grasp why it was happening—where the bizarre images planted in the back of my mind sprouted from—my uncle would be able to explain and assure me I wasn't hallucinating, and that's why Jennings mailed the photos to him. Or was I giving Jennings too much credit? After all, my uncle was in his late fifties, and what if he died before I had these obscene visions? As much as I disliked the overused phrase: *Don't Worry*, I loathed the never-ending question: *What If?* I didn't want to lead my life full of what-ifs. Instead, I liked to fill my head with hope. I hoped Jake Jennings had hope. I hoped for his final actions… his life-after-death experience would be one of redemption—he would be forgiven for assisting his dad and keeping quiet.

I hoped Jake Jennings intentionally wanted to make it clear to my uncle that including the negatives was his way of reassuring him that this was the end—no one would ever get a hold of the photos. I hoped this made Jake Jennings rest in peace, especially after what Betsy had told me—what might have happened to him as a child by his own dad. I thanked God I had amazing parents. And for the first time, I thanked God they were together in heaven. This would have crushed them if they were alive, especially since they were the ones who organized my drop-offs at Mr. Jennings Senior's home, waving good-bye to me as the old man, who always dressed up as Old Saint Nick at the company's Christmas party, led me to his sex chamber disguised as Fun Land.

I tried not to feel empty. Empty as the bowl of spare change that sat on my dad's bureau after he let me grab handfuls of coins and run outside when I heard the ring-a-ring of the ice cream truck slowly trickling down my street. *Will I ever look at strawberry ice cream in the same way?* That delicious treat I loved as a child, knowing it was what lured me into Mr. Jennings's trap? At the center of myself in an aching hole, knowing what Mr. Jennings Senior did to me, and even though it was my mom who took the picture, Cooper admired so much, I knew I wouldn't be able to look at it with the same admiration.

After a long silence as we sat in the kitchen trying to finish our now cold breakfast, I said, looking in my uncle's direction, "Don't be surprised if Pamela calls you soon."

"Huh? Why?"

"Pamela will need your legal counsel."

"What are you talking about?" My uncle asked.

"Last night, Michaels showed me photos that were confiscated when they searched another perv's home—they were of Alexis. He didn't know it until he came over Thanksgiving and recognized her."

"Oh, my God. Did he say if he was going to go in person or were they going to call Pamela in?"

"He didn't say. But I wouldn't be surprised if she calls you immediately after finding out."

"Oh my God," was all he said.

CHAPTER 22
CONFIDING IN LUCKY

On my drive back to my dorm, I asked myself whether I was going to tell Luke and Amber Lee? Probably. When? I didn't know. Was I going to tell Lucky, Jezebel, and Gloria? I wasn't sure if I wanted to. Gloria—I could avoid. Lucky, I couldn't. He was on top of me like a barn cat on a mouse and would pick up that something was wrong. Jezebel shared similar discernment, but she didn't pry as much as Lucky. She was also barely in our room when I was there these days. Other than French Immersion, her class schedule didn't coincide with mine, and paths only really crossed at parties. I'd find her inebriated and dancing with a group of girls in the middle of the room or tucked on the sofa with some hottie making out.

Lucky had spotted me the minute I got out of my car in the student parking lot and pounced.

Practically shouting, "Where have you been? You missed Art History! And we talked about Andy Warhol—the soup legend!" he still managed to joke, although he was panting, leaning his hands against the hood to catch his breath.

"Sorry," was all I said.

"Sorry? Sorry? That's it?"

I just shrugged my shoulders and began walking. He followed.

"When I came to get you for breakfast and found you weren't in your room, I got worried. But just assumed you went for a run. But then, when you weren't in Art History—your favorite class, I said to myself—something's wrong. So, what is it? What is so wrong that you missed class?"

We had reached my room, and I made sure Lucky had shut the door behind us before I told him. My voice started slow, but then something weird came over me—I felt like I was being timed and was only given sixty seconds to shout out the right answers as if I were on a game show. I talked quickly, with my Italian hands! The words tumbled out faster and faster until I was breathless and had nothing left to tell, as I fell back onto my bed and covered my face with my hands, trying to abstain from crying, which was impossible.

Lucky was quiet for the first time.

CHAPTER 23
JUST A DREAM

There was a strange white light. I thought it might be like being one of the sepulchers from the Bible. The strong sunlight was cut down by the wall in front of the doorway, and a pearly beam fell on the sides and floor. I summoned his image… Jake Jennings stood to the side—his big, black, professional-looking camera hung around his neck. Mr. Jennings Senior stood a yard away from me, holding a double-scoop cone, *Strawberry*, he said. A smile started slowly at the corners of his mouth and grew until it lit up his entire, wrinkled, tanned face. *Your favorite, Dakota!*

I sat up in stark fear, awoken from this strange and perverse dream, thinking I had heard a puppy's whine outside my door. I ran to it and opened it only to find a dimly lit, empty corridor—no puppy at my feet.

"Dakota! Oh my God! You're having another one of your dreams!" Jezebel rapidly spewed while hurrying to shut the door. She then lightly nudged me into her bed and hushed me back to sleep.

***

"Sometimes they were worse," I told the group. The support group Betsy encouraged me to attend; I had asked Lucky if he would come with me—he didn't hesitate. The group was for victims of sex crimes. The woman across from me, who was twirling a long piece of her jet-black hair, seemed strange. She was the first to comment and asked me a series of questions all at once before letting me answer the first one.

"Like what? How is it worse? Was there blood? Did you have a weapon? Did you kill him?" She sounded more mechanical than concerned and empathetic.

I thought we were supposed to be good listeners, supportive, and ask appropriate questions—that could help. But this woman wanted gory details as if she had planned to write a script for a horror show.

"It was only a dream," I answered.

The strange woman looked disappointed.

"Tell us another one," the group leader encouraged. The other eight nodded.

Lucky was the only one who said, resting his hand on my knee, "You don't have to if you don't want to."

"Oh yes, of course, you don't have to, but it may help. We may be able to help you through it. You know—figure it out," the group leader said with a slight smile and then looked at Lucky as if he were a troublemaker.

"I've had images of me swimming naked in a pool—an opulent pool one would expect to see in a king's palace," I spoke softly. I was feeling painfully embarrassed, even though the group leader always started us off after our unison prayer, reminding us that none of us should ever feel embarrassed by our words during our ninety-minute session together. *We are a family*, she'd say, and then ask, *Who would like to start?*

"The king is Mr. Jennings. The pool is Mr. Jennings'," the woman who twirled her hair repeatedly. "Didn't you tell us he had a pool? Naturally, he lost the swimsuit your mom packed and convinced you it was all right to swim naked. He probably told you some cockamamie story." Then she examined the ends of her hair she had coiled on one finger. "Ugh, dead ends. I need to get myself a haircut."

Lucky looked in her direction and said curtly, "Must be nice to have all the answers."

I don't think what he had said registered with her because she didn't rebut it. She seemed very much out there.

The middle-aged woman who wore a dark-colored, smock-like dress that covered her feet when she sat, said in almost a whisper, "God must have an achy back," as she thumbed the wooden crucifix that hung around her neck, which looked like it was strung with a sneaker shoelace.

"What'd she say?" asked a dark skin woman who was dressed just the opposite—her too-tight dress hardly covered her flabby thighs and large bosoms. Then she yelled, "What'd you say, woman?"

The crucifix woman became nervous and said nothing, looking down at her lap.

The group leader answered for her. She said, looking confused, "God must have an achy back?"

"What in the hell is wrong with you, woman?" flabby thighs cried.

"Or a strong back," the young Amish-looking man interrupted.

All of us just looked at him. He rarely spoke.

He continued, "What I think she was trying to explain to all of us is that God must have a strong back because he carries all the weight of the world." Then, looking at the lady wearing the crucifix, who had slowly lifted her head, he finished, "We are thankful God is mighty strong." He smiled.

The lady looked at him with kind eyes and said, "God bless you, son."

A guy dressed in Army fatigues said, "Amen."

I wondered if he subconsciously wore camouflage clothing to mask his inner fears, pretending to have been in the military, because he did not strike me as the kind who'd enlist.

"Thank you for sharing, Dakota." Then, as if she were working behind a deli counter, the group leader called, "Next!"

CHAPTER 24
WINTER BREAK

Christmas was just around the corner. I couldn't wait to see Savannah's face when she saw what Santa had brought her. Luke had been working on it for months, keeping it at his work in case she found it at home. It was a Victorian dollhouse—the one she wanted in some toy catalog,

When I'd shown it to him, he laughed, "That? I can make that for half the price and better! I bet that thing's made of fake wood and will fall apart after one week of playing with it. But if I make it—it'll be of quality, and last a lifetime—passed onto my grandbabies!"

I laughed. Couldn't believe he was already thinking of when he'd be a grandpa!

"Okay. Be my guest, but I'd start on it now. There are a lot of intricate details! Just look at that staircase's carved banister," I said, pointing to the picture that took up most of the page.

"Mine will be better," he cried as he took the catalog from my hand, rolled it up, and put it in his back pocket. "I'm off to the lumber yard," he called halfway out the door.

"Good luck!" I cried as I smiled, thinking how much he reminded me of our dad.

I just hoped he was better at building things than Dad. The tree house Dad had patched together was considered unsafe by Mom's standards within the first month of its unveiling! Dad blamed it on the fluke week-long rainstorm Fort Worth experienced that year, and Mom argued with sass, *"Noah's boat lasted for forty days without a ladder falling off!"*

It was going to be Teddy's first Christmas, too. And like everything else, Amber Lee wanted to make it perfect—everything decorated down to a tee. She had even found an ornament to present to Savannah the day we put up the tree. Amber Lee told her to close her eyes and put out her hands as she placed a glass bulb that had

First Christmas as Big Sister painted in gold cursive. When Savannah opened her eyes, her smile was as bright as the lights on the tree.

Teddy had already received at least half a dozen ornaments from friends and family that were all so different yet held the same significance—his first Christmas. My favorite was the simple pewter teddy bear that had Teddy's date of birth engraved on its rump.

As I finished the last of the synthetic evergreen garland, wrapping it around the posts of the entrance to the stable, Detective Michaels pulled up.

Before even shutting his car door, he called, "Oh, good, you're here!"

I folded the stepladder closed. "Hey! What's up?" I asked.

We walked into the barn, where I rested the stepladder.

"Dakota, about the other night."

"You mean three weeks ago?" I said, walking over to the horses. All three of their heads peered out of their stalls as if wanting to listen in on our conversation.

"Has it been that long?"

"Yes, it has." I handed him a sugar cube from my pocket and gently directed, "Here, make yourself useful. Give St. Patty a treat. I've got Merry and Christmas."

"Which one is yours?" he asked as he laid his palm flat for St. Patty to mouth the sugar cube. Then he patted his head, sweetly saying, "That a boy."

"Christmas is mine. Merry belongs to Savannah."

"Let me guess, you got 'em for Christmas? And Luke got his on Saint Patrick's Day?"

"Half right. St. Patty was born on the holiday. He came with his name. Luke liked it and kept it," I said, turning away and opening the next box of decorations. Wreaths made of the same synthetic evergreens were inside with red velvet bows already attached. I began looping the wreaths through my arm. I gestured to where the tools were hanging, "Grab that hammer for me, please."

"I'm sorry if I upset you," Michaels said, walking to where the hammer hung. "I just assumed you wanted to be in the loop."

I grabbed a handful of nails from an old Tupperware.

"Dakota, what did Jake mean when he apologized for what he and his dad did?"

I only shrugged my shoulders and busied myself with the wreaths.

"The cops put it to rest, but it doesn't add up," he said.

"It doesn't matter anymore," I said.

"They cleared Jake's property. It's no longer part of the investigation," he said.

"So? What do I care about his stupid penthouse?" I barked. "And the investigation is over. His case was put to rest."

"He didn't own that. He rented. I'm talking about his dad's estate—where Jake grew up. It's up for auction."

My heart sank, but I didn't want to give away my look of alarm—what could they have found? I tried to act levelheaded. "Yeah? So, you're thinking of buying it?" I asked smart-alecky, turning away from him. I banged a nail into the wall next to Merry's stall, hanging the first barn wreath.

"Nice," Michaels said, admiring how perfectly the name was centered in the middle of the wreath. "And no. I couldn't afford it. It'd be nice, though. The place is beautiful."

"Gross," I said aloud. Then wishing I hadn't.

"Gross?"

"Yeah, it was the home of a criminal," I said, backpedaling.

"Jake became scandalous after his dad died nine years ago," Michaels said, defending the manor as if the structure had feelings.

I remembered going to Mr. Jennings Senior's funeral with my dad. My mom tried, but she was too sick. Her skinny body concaved as she dry heaved into the large stainless-steel bowl that sat by her bedside, and in between sighs, she asked us to say an extra prayer for him from her. Dad didn't want to go. He was fearful of leaving her alone. But my mother insisted. *Please, Jethro, we owe the man that much. After all that he's done for this family.*

"I did a walk-through," Michaels said.

"Cool." *What in the hell was he leading to?* I was really getting annoyed with his guilelessness.

"He had a dark room in his basement. Did you know he was a photographer?"

I shook my head, now holding a nail between my lips, as I was getting ready to hammer in the next Christmas wreath.

"Well, he did. It had some vintage equipment, too, which was able to produce these. He was quite a fan of yours!" He smiled, reaching into the breast pocket of his camel hair jacket, and pulled out a business letter-sized envelope. And from that, he pulled out about a dozen small black and white photos—the old-fashioned square-sized photos that are no longer produced.

I inwardly prayed, *Please be clothed, Dakota. Please be clothed.*

He held one up. "This is my favorite," he said, smiling, showing it to me.

It was similar to the one my mom had taken of me after I had devoured an ice cream cone This one showed my tongue licking around a dripping cone.

"What flavor?" he chuckled.

I felt like the floor just gave out. Michaels grabbed hold of me.

"Dakota? Are you all right?" he asked, catching me in mid-stream. He dropped the photos. I pushed him off and slid to the floor rapidly spreading the photos apart, and examining each one. Michaels knelt next to me, alarmed at my reaction, and pleaded, "Dakota? What's wrong?"

"Was this all you found? Were there more?" I asked in a frenzy, picking a photo, looking for clues, dropping it, picking up another, and repeating the task as if time was running out and my life depended on it.

"Yeah. Calm down, Dakota."

"Why in the hell do you have to act so Goddamn weird when you find things?" I said anxiously.

"Me, weird?" he said as I was still examining each photo closely—wishing I had a magnifying glass.

"I thought they were sweet photos. I thought it'd be nice to show you. They're of you and your family at some big party he threw!"

"It was his annual Memorial Day barbecue!" I practically yelled.

"Dakota, I'm sorry. I didn't mean to upset you. It seems like I'm becoming an expert at that."

I chuckled, but I wasn't laughing at his quip. I was laughing like a crazy person, relieved none of these photos were pornographic.

He pointed to one of my uncles, "Travis looked thirty pounds lighter back then." Then he pointed to another and asked, "Is this your mom?"

I nodded.

"She's beautiful. You look like her."

"Thanks," I smiled and then, finding one of Dad, I said, "And this is my dad." A German shepherd was sitting by him.

"Is that your dog?" he asked. "Great breed. I had a mutt growing up."

"No. It was the Jennings'," I answered, but only because I remembered what my uncle had told me. I had no recollection of the animal from childhood.

"Here he is, Mr. Jennings, holding you. I guess Jake was the one with the camera—he's not in any of these."

"Yeah, I guess so," I said, staring at the wrinkly, old face and noticing his hands were under my dress while he held me on his hip.

"It's tragic how Jake turned out," Michaels commented. "Looks like his dad was a nice guy. Sure, threw a fun party. Even had a trampoline for the kids to play on," Detective Michaels said, pointing to one of the photos where Jake was able to capture me in mid-air as I bounced.

"Looks can be deceiving," I mumbled.

Thankfully, he ignored my remark.

"I've had enough 'memory lane' for now." I gathered the photos up, put them back in the envelope, and pushed them down into the back pocket of my Levi's. "Thanks," I said. "I'll be sure to show the fam!"

I walked him out to his car.

"Dakota, you have yourself a very merry Christmas. You deserve it."

"Thanks. You too. Are you going anywhere?" I asked, just to ease my mind, that he wouldn't be popping in for another surprise visit.

He smiled, "Yes, visiting my sister and her two kids in Colorado."

"Great. Well, safe travels," was all I said.

At the moment, I really didn't want to learn about his sister. If she was older or younger than him, how old her kids were, if he liked being an uncle, and if he was a cool one. It's not that I didn't care. I just wasn't in the mood to talk to him anymore. Maybe I'd call him after Christmas break, and we could meet at Willy's, and I could ask what kinds of fun things he did with his sister's kids and what he got them for Christmas. We gave each other a hearty goodbye hug, but before he released me completely, he kissed my cheek and told me to be good.

I laughed, "I always am!"

He chuckled while getting into his car.

I smiled, inwardly thinking it was about time I heard him laugh. Then he was on his merry way.

I stayed in the drive watching his car grow smaller as he sped away. I was glad he had a family to go to for the holiday. Uncle Travis was coming here a few days before Christmas and staying till the New Year. He had tried to persuade Betsy to go someplace exotic with him, but she said she was too busy finishing up her doctoral thesis. She was motivated to earn her degree and anxious to get her practice up and running. Betsy had a positive effect on my uncle. He had started watching what he ate, cutting back on red meat, and began exercising, too.

***

Savannah was excitedly hopping about as if her feet were on fire, looking at the kitchen clock even though she couldn't tell the time. She was anxiously waiting for her baby brother to wake up from his nap. Amber Lee was taking them to the mall to have their picture taken with Santa Claus.

"I can't wait! I can't wait!" Savannah bellowed.

"You look so pretty," I said, admiring her emerald green velvet dress with a lace collar.

She slid around the kitchen's freshly waxed floor in her stocking-covered feet as if she were ice-skating. She was singing 'Santa Claus Is Coming To Town'. I immediately took out my iPhone to take a video of her. I even captured her black patent leather shoes perfectly placed by the door. Within moments, Amber Lee strode down holding Teddy, who wore a romper the same color as Savannah's dress, minus the lace collar. Naturally, what Amber Lee wore complemented her children's apparel: emerald green slacks with an ivory-colored blouse and black patent leather flats. Her striding in three-inch heels was reserved for date nights.

That evening, I offered to babysit so Luke and Amber Lee could attend a Christmas party that Luke's bookkeeper was throwing. Amber Lee went over the list she wrote as if I couldn't read, but I stayed quiet and nodded, taking in all the common-sense instructions. I imagined, like many new moms, she was nervous about leaving her baby, even though she trusted me one hundred percent. Standing behind her, Luke had mouthed 'thank you' to me while clasping his hands, looking like an altar boy. It was hard not to laugh, but I knew if I had, Amber Lee would chide us for making fun of her.

"I'm sure the three or four hours you guys are gone, Teddy will remain asleep, so you have nothing to worry about. Now go on and have a good time. I've got the fort. And you look beautiful by the way, but then again, you always do, Amber Lee."

She changed into a very flattering fitted red dress with matching shoes and a scarf with a Christmas motif of candy canes and gingerbread men. She thanked me and air kissed me—not wanting to smudge her lipstick. Her scarf had given me the idea to make gingerbread cookies with Savannah.

I had the medley of Perry Como, Bing Crosby, and Nat King Cole's Christmas songs playing in the background as we rolled out the dough and cut snowmen, stars, fir trees, and gingerbread men. Afterward, we watched the classic Christmas movie, *Rudolph the Red-Nosed Reindeer*, and then, as we snuggled in Savannah's bed, I read the classics: *The Night Before Christmas* and *Frosty the Snowman*. It didn't take long before she fell asleep as I tiptoed out of her room to finish cleaning up the mess we had made decorating the cookies—I needed to sweep up the sprinkles and red and green colored sugar that dusted the floor.

It was nearing eleven when Uncle Travis pulled in. I was glad Luke and Amber Lee were still out having a good time. My uncle let himself in.

"Oh, sweet heaven—it smells delicious," he said as he moseyed over to the counter that looked like it belonged in the display window of a bakery. He eyed them all and then nabbed a snowman and bit off its head before hugging me!

I offered, "There's plenty. Bring some to Betsy."

He gasped, "Don't tell her I ate a cookie!"

I laughed, "Boy, does she have you whipped!"

"She's dead set against eating past eight!"

"Well, it's working, cause you look like you've lost at least five pounds."

"Eight!" he boasted, "and twelve more to go."

"Awesome!"

"So, Betsy tells me you're attending some group."

"I have a few times, but I think I'm going to stop."

"Why?"

"I don't think I have much to share. During the times I have gone, I only had my strange dreams to tell them about, but thankfully, those stopped. It's as if a dark cloud moved away from me."

"Closure," he said.

"Yeah. Closure," I repeated.

"Sometimes my mother visits me in my dreams," he said.

"Yeah?" I said, sounding surprised. My uncle rarely mentioned his mom.

"Yup. She asks me what I've done with this," he said, pulling a small, gray, felt jewelry box from his pocket. "It belonged to my mother. I've been waiting for someone special to give it to."

Before even seeing it, I blurted, "I'm sure Betsy will love it!"

"Shush," my uncle teased, "let me finish." He slowly revealed a gold necklace. "Of course, I always knew it was you I wanted to give it to, but you just weren't mature enough—not of the right age, I mean—to appreciate it. But now I know you are."

Tears welled in my eyes as quickly as one could count to three.

When it came into full view, I could see the gold chain holding something tiny. I looked closer, holding my uncle's hand steady. There was a small, delicate gold bird with light blue eyes.

"It's beautiful," I gasped. "Are you sure you want to part with it?"

"Her eyes are topaz," he said, smiling, "and her body—eighteen carat gold." He then took it from its box and gently ordered me to turn around. "Besides, as long as I have you, I'll always have it." My back was facing him as he tried fastening the gold chain around my neck with great effort. "How in the world do women do this?" Then, as he managed to open the clasp, he said, "There we go! Phew! Now turn around and let me see."

I smiled.

"Beautiful," he said. Then, looking up at the ceiling for a quick second, he smiled, "My mother thinks so too."

I stepped to the small mirror that hung in the mudroom off the kitchen to admire what once belonged to his mother. I felt deeply touched.

"I love it!" I exclaimed, touching the bird that perfectly nestled in the hollow of my neck.

"My mother hadn't much jewelry—real, that is. My dad couldn't afford it, but I remember the look on her face the Christmas he had given this to her—the year no kids were living at home."

"I get it. Your parents were empty nesters. Cute!"

He smiled and delicately tapped the gold bird, "But I think for you, this little guy can symbolize many things."

I returned the smile. "My mom did love Barbra Streisand's 'Songbird'."

"I remember. She liked all her songs."

"And there is a type of sparrow called Savannah!" I said, sounding excited as if this was a guessing game and I was getting all the answers right.

"The Savannah bird is what I had thought of initially… although I love the correlation with your mom."

"Uncle Travis, I love it. Thank you so much. I love you! You're the best uncle in the whole wide world!"

He chuckled, "My sentiments exactly. And you, my dear, the apple of my eye, are the perfect person my mom would want this to be passed down to. She was a believer in stoic women. And you personify that beautifully."

After our heartfelt hug, the two of us moved to the living room where the ginormous tree stood, beautifully decorated with tiny white lights, red bulbs, and a plethora of store-bought and homemade ornaments. I flicked the switch to turn on the gas-burning fireplace. We both sat next to each other on the sofa.

"I'm proud of you, Dakota," my uncle said, holding my hand.

"Thanks." And then I kidded, "I'm proud of you, too!"

He smiled. "So, I hear you're spending a few days in Boston with Cooper."

"Yeah, who told you?"

"I can't reveal my sources, but she's awfully cute."

"Savannah! How'd she know?"

"Cooper told her."

We laughed, and I was relieved he didn't seem upset. "What are you and Betsy doing for the New Year?"

"She has to work at Rhonda's. I told Luke he could take Amber Lee out for dinner, and I'd babysit."

"What?" I guffawed. "Are you sure you can handle it?"

"I want to learn."

"What? You want to learn?"

"Yup! Got it all figured out. I'm going to stay home and take care of the kids while my wife tackles her career. You know, be one of those twenty-first-century stay-at-home dads!"

"What?" I wasn't sure if he was kidding or not.

"Dakota, I think I want to retire—sell my practice... and raise a family."

"Oh, my God! Are you serious?"

"Yes."

"Does Betsy know?"

"She's the career woman I'm talking about. Of course, she knows!"

I was completely smitten. "Holy Cow! When in the world did you have this revelation?" I cried. And then, looking up, I cooed, "Thank you, Lord!"

"Betsy told me she didn't want to be an old mom—she wants a kid by the time she's thirty, but she also wants a career. She wants two kids!" He put up two of his fingers and added with a smile, "Two years apart! She reminded me that she didn't just spend all those years in college just to put her degree to rest, but also didn't want to put her babies in daycare. So it'd be awesome if her husband were willing to stay home the first few years of their lives! Of course, he would have to be madly in love with her and dote on her too, while being a fun-loving, but know-when-to-discipline-type-dad!"

"Wow! She said all that?"

Uncle Travis nodded.

"Betsy knows what she wants! So how do you fit in?"

"She told me she loves me."

"Do you love her?"

"When she told me she loved me, I didn't take her seriously. All the women in my life have told me that, Dakota. I'm not trying to brag, but really, it sounded as if it was just tongue-in-cheek. Love's easy to say. So, Betsy looked into my eyes—stared for a long, hard moment, and told me I was the one! Me? Can you imagine? Of course, I joked with her, reminding her how old I was and could pass as her dad. But she doesn't care."

"I thought when Pamela told you she wanted another kid, you said you were too old to father a child?"

"That's what I thought until I met Betsy."

"So, you do love her?"

"Very much.", Uncle Travis said with a smile. "And I don't believe in having a kid out of wedlock intentionally, even though it is widely accepted in today's society. There are certain values where I'm a traditionalist at heart ."

"That's what my mom loved about you."

He smiled.

"So how are you going to propose?"

He chuckled, "We're already engaged!"

"What?"

"She proposed to me!"

"What?" I laughed. "How?"

"She was at her computer and said, 'I'm ordering five hundred business cards, and I need to know if they should read Elizabeth Mary O'Brian or Elizabeth O'Brian Kenwood.'"

I laughed, "Really?"

"Yes! Took me completely by surprise, but honestly, Dakota, I loved it."

I smiled. "So, what'd you tell her?"

"I told her to keep it simple. Have them read Dr. Betsy Kenwood."

I was smiling so much that my cheeks were beginning to hurt. "You'll make an exceptional husband and father."

"Thank you, darlin'."

"And Betsy will equally match it by being a loving mom and a wife no husband would tire of."

"Oh yeah. She'll definitely keep me young!"

"And your kids will help with that too!" I laughed.

Uncle Travis beamed.

"Hey, I know how you can get your feet wet! Come to church with me tomorrow to help Mrs. White and the reverend with the kids. There's still a lot more to do with the children's Christmas pageant before the twenty-fifth when Savannah plays the Virgin Mary."

"Okay."

"Okay? Just like that?"

"Yup!" He answered, taking hold of my hand, and repeated, "Just like that!"

I gave it three squeezes, which was my code for *I Love You.*

He returned two... which was code for *Me Too.*

I have always maintained hope that my uncle would eventually settle down, and on this night, it just paid off.

ACKNOWLEDGEMENT

I would like to sincerely thank the many friends, colleagues, acquaintances, gym buddies, and family members who supported my writing journey every step of the way. Your constant reminders that publishing a book is a tremendous achievement—and that I somehow managed to publish three—never failed to make me smile. Your amazement, encouragement, and pride meant more to me than you may ever know.

I am especially grateful to those who took the time to read *Because of Savannah* and *Dakota*, and who went the extra mile to write thoughtful reviews. Your generosity, enthusiasm, and belief in my work gave me the motivation to keep going. And now, here you are again, embarking on *Lucky*, the third and final installment of this journey.

Thank you for cheering me on, believing in me, and helping bring these stories into the world. I could not have done this without you.